Oh, come in! Welcome to the Witch's House Café. ♥

Slime Spirit (Big Sister)
Falfa

Slime Spirit (Little Sister)
Shalsha

High-ranking Demon
Beelzebub

Elf Apothecary
Halkara

Red Dragon–Girl

Laika

The Witch of the Highlands

Azusa

If you want to save the elf's life, you must fight me—Demon King Pecora!

I've Been Killing SLIMES for 300 Years and Maxed Out My Level ❷

Kisetsu Morita

Illustration by Benio

YEN ON

NEW YORK

I've Been Killing SLIMES for 300 Years and Maxed Out My Level 2

KISETSU MORITA

Translation by Taylor Engel

Cover art by Benio

SLIME TAOSHITE SANBYAKUNEN, SHIRANAIUCHINI
LEVEL MAX NI NATTEMASHITA vol. 2
Copyright © 2017 Kisetsu Morita
Illustrations copyright © 2017 Benio
All rights reserved.
Original Japanese edition published in 2017 by SB Creative Corp.

This English edition is published by arrangement with SB Creative Corp., Tokyo
in care of Tuttle-Mori Agency, Inc., Tokyo.

English translation © 2018 by Yen Press, LLC

Yen On
1290 Avenue of the Americas
New York, NY 10104

Visit us at yenpress.com
facebook.com/yenpress
twitter.com/yenpress
yenpress.tumblr.com
instagram.com/yenpress

First Yen On Edition: August 2018

Yen On is an imprint of Yen Press, LLC.
The Yen On name and logo are trademarks of Yen Press, LLC.

Library of Congress Cataloging-in-Publication Data
Names: Morita, Kisetsu, author. | Benio, illustrator. | Engel, Taylor, translator.
Title: I've been killing slimes for 300 years and maxed out my level / Kisetsu Morita ;
illustration by Benio ; translation by Taylor Engel.
Other titles: Slime taoshite sanbyakunen, shiranaiuchini level max ni nattemashita. English |
I have been killing slimes for 300 years
Description: First Yen On edition. | New York : Yen On, 2018–
Identifiers: LCCN 2017059843 | ISBN 9780316448277 (v. 1 : pbk.) | ISBN 9780316448291 (v. 2 : pbk.)
Subjects: CYAC: Reincarnation—Fiction. | Witches—Fiction.
Classification: LCC PZ7.1.M6725 Iv 2018 | DDC [Fic]—dc23
LC record available at https://lccn.loc.gov/2017059843

ISBNs: 978-0-316-44829-1 (paperback)
978-0-316-44830-7 (ebook)

1 3 5 7 9 10 8 6 4 2

LSC-C

Printed in the United States of America

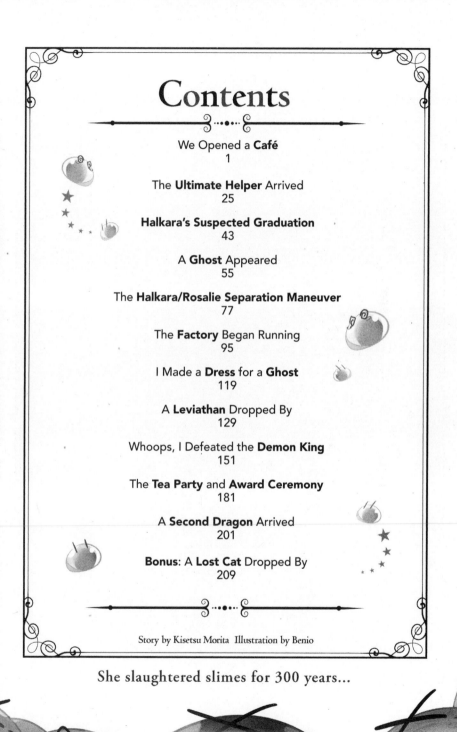

Contents

Story by Kisetsu Morita   Illustration by Benio

She slaughtered slimes for 300 years...

Three hundred years after coming to this new world, for the first time in my life, I'd fought with dragons.

We returned to the highland cottage in high spirits.

"Mmm! It really is nice to be home!"

I almost never took overnight trips, so this was a fairly novel feeling.

"The bride was pretty, wasn't she, Mommy?"

Although there had been trouble at the wedding—particularly the blue dragon attack—Falfa already seemed to consider it a fun memory. What an excellent attitude.

"You're right. Laika's big sister looked happy."

"If I have a wedding someday, I wonder if I'll be able to wear a dress like hers."

Falfa's comment was innocent enough—but I froze up a little.

"When I get married, I want to live in a cute redbrick house."

D-does that mean she'll leave this one?!

"F-Falfa... You know, even after you're married, you and your husband could live here. We could build another addition, make it a two-family home..."

"What are you talking about, Mommy?"

Falfa tilted her head, looking blank. *Oh, good. She isn't thinking about marriage in concrete terms yet. Phew, I'm safe!*

Just then, Shalsha patted me on the back.

"Shalsha wants to stay with you forever, Mom. I've been learning how to cook lately. I want you to eat delicious meals."

Oh, Shalsha's trying to make me feel better!

I hugged her in spite of myself. My girls were so precious it hurt.

As a mother, I made sure to hug my daughters as an essential part of my child-rearing philosophy.

"Mom, did that make you happy?"

Shalsha was a reserved child who didn't generally let her emotions show on her face, but inside, she was incredibly kind. I knew that very well.

"Yes, of course. Your feelings got through to me, Shalsha."

"Just Shalsha?! No fair! Hug Falfa, too, Mommy! Hug me tight!"

Falfa begged, bouncing up and down.

Falfa was true to her own feelings, but she was just as tender and considerate as her little sister, Shalsha. Of course, I loved them both the same—infinitely.

"Yes, yes. Your mother wouldn't be unfair about these things."

This time I squeezed Falfa tightly.

"All right, why don't the three of us sleep together as a family tonight? It's been a long time."

"Yaaaaay! Falfa's happy!"

Shalsha nodded as well.

I wouldn't trade a chance for a nap with my daughters for several billion yen. I wouldn't budge an inch on that.

Just then, I felt eyes on us. Right away, I knew it was Laika and Halkara looking at us.

True, if I gave my daughters too much special treatment, the others would get jealous.

A short while ago at the volcano, I'd told Laika that she was like a little sister to me, and since she looked as if she'd just started middle school, the comparison was apt.

Halkara was a slightly flaky apprentice, but although the word *apprentice* was usually written with the character for *little brother* in my language, there was no reason you couldn't make up a feminine form that used the character for *little sister*. So, with a little tweaking of the definition, I could think of her as a younger sister, too.

"Wait just a second," I told my daughters, turning away from them. I went up to my two little sisters and pointedly ruffled their hair.

"Honestly! You mustn't look so left out. Come on, none of that!"

"Lady Azusa, you'll mess up my hair… Although…I don't really mind…"

The ever-serious Laika expressed her feelings hesitantly.

This house in the highlands wasn't where any of them were from, after all. I intended to actively support them, to keep them from getting lonesome.

On the other hand, Halkara clung to me of her own accord. Somehow, it reminded me of when I was in high school. Some of the girls had been weirdly clingy then, too.

However, in Halkara's case, there was a physical obstacle to closeness.

Boyoing.

I knew it. Her chest was touching me.

"Hmm…? I can't quite seem to get close to you. Why is that?"

She's actually wondering. I think she should be a bit more conscious of how buxom she really is…

"I wonder if I could borrow a little of your bust… Is there a spell for that?"

"Did you say something, Madam Teacher?"

"…No. Nothing."

And so our family trip to Mount Rokko for Laika's older sister's wedding ended without further mishap. Flatorte, the blue dragons' former leader, had quieted down considerably after Beelzebub glared at her, so there probably wouldn't be any retaliation.

That was why I thought we'd fall back into our daily routine in earnest, but—

"Lady Azusa, I'll need to begin the dinner preparations soon. However, as I didn't go shopping before our journey, we don't have many ingredients on hand," Laika reported.

And we were a large family, too. If I had her go shopping now, though, the vegetables and things might be sold out already.

"In that case, why don't we all eat in the village today?"

◇

As usual, we made for the village at a leisurely walk, but we did do a little work along the way.

In this family, "work" meant exterminating slimes. They turned up on the road to the village, so we made sure to take them all out.

"If you spot a slime, kill it and retrieve its magic stone, all right?"

To cover the cost of dining out for a party of five, I needed to kill at least twenty-five. Each one generated a magic stone that was worth two hundred gold, which was roughly equivalent to two hundred Japanese yen.

The restaurants in the village weren't too fancy, so we could eat there for about a thousand gold per person. However, taking the cost of drinks and things into account, it wouldn't hurt to kill a few more. It wasn't that we were hard up for money, but I liked to earn what I used in a day before the day was over.

"Even *I* can kill slimes."

Halkara was hitting the springy monsters as though it was a sort of exercise.

However, Falfa checked her.

"Big Sister Halkara, that's a good slime, so you mustn't kill it."

"Huh? This one is?"

"Uh-huh. The slime over there is a bad one, so you should kill it. Look, see those two over there? It's the puffy-looking one."

"Um, this one?"

"Not that one! That one's good, too!"

"It's hard to tell them apart…"

I wasn't really sure how and where good slimes differed from bad ones yet, myself.

"Halkara, pale slimes are bad. The deeper-colored slimes are good. Just remember that."

"I understand what you're saying, Shalsha, but it's not exactly easy to distinguish color depth."

Timidly, Halkara killed the next slime.

After about half an hour of work, our family had managed to rack up a total of thirty-eight slimes.

By my estimation, we'd probably recouped the cost of our meal at the restaurant.

When we reached the village of Flatta, people were putting up decorations for some reason.

Colorful cloths hung on the walls, and the village's main street looked rather bright and festive.

"Oh, that's right. It's almost time for the Dance Festival."

I'd remembered that it was just about that time of year.

The Dance Festival was a traditional festival of the village of Flatta. I say "traditional," but back when I first came to live here, they hadn't started it yet.

They held the first one about two hundred and fifty years ago, and it had stuck around ever since. As far as normal people were concerned, once something went on for two hundred and fifty years, it counted as tradition.

"Lady Azusa, what manner of festival is it?"

Laika hadn't seen it before, so she didn't know.

"People dance in the village square and in the highlands whenever they want to, any way they like. Of course, there are street stalls as well, so you can have fun even if you don't dance."

"Ah. So this is a custom of your culture? How intriguing."

"Calling it a cultural custom makes it sound really formal, but it's a laid-back festival. I hear it was originally for the time when people offered the fruits of their harvest to an earth deity and asked for continued blessings in the coming year, but almost no one pays attention to that now."

Exercise burned off stress, too. By dancing all day, you built up the energy to give it your best in other tasks later.

"Oh, if it isn't the great Witch and company." The man from the shop where we always bought our butter hailed us. He was in the middle of hanging colorful fabric on a wall, too.

"Good afternoon. It's almost time for the festival, isn't it?"

"That's right. Say, would you do something for the festival as well, great Witch? We'd gladly welcome your contribution. Although, naturally, we'd be happy even if you came to look around like always."

"Mm, yes. But you know, I try not to participate in the actual festival. If I did, I might end up leading it…"

In a word, the village would be in danger of losing its autonomy.

After all, I was a witch who'd been living there since before the festival began. If such a being took part in the festival, the villagers would be left unable to say anything.

I'd hate to end up feeling like I was dominating the village, so I'd stuck to my stance of abstaining from the festival program.

However, this year, my circumstances were a bit different.

"If it's a festival, do you think they'll have stalls selling candy?!"

"It's possible to discern the nature of villagers through their festival rites. Research of tradition is important to the study of history as well."

Falfa and Shalsha were showing interest… Although they found their interest in very different things.

"A festival, hmm? At elvish festivals, I made money selling exclusive drinks. When I offered a plant-based elixir that prevented hangovers, it just flew off the shelf. Maybe I'll sell it again. At festivals, your products will sell even if at high prices; it's quite an easy business."

Halkara's thoughts were also turning toward the festival, although hers were less than pure.

Laika was glancing at the preparations, too.

Well, my family had expanded rapidly. Maybe I could take this opportunity to try changing how I was involved with the festival.

That said, presenting as a family would be a tall order, and if we ended up being completely tied to our part of it, we wouldn't have the freedom to enjoy the festival normally. That would completely defeat the purpose.

Was there some kind of decent compromise?

"Great Witch, there's a celebration the day before the festival as well. You could do something then instead," the butter man said.

"That's true. If we did that, it wouldn't overlap with the main festival, but… Hmm…"

I couldn't come up with an answer immediately, so for the moment, I shelved the matter.

We went to my favorite restaurant, the Savvy Eagle, for a grand dinner.

Roast duck was on the menu this time of year, and it had been exquisitely seasoned. I wasn't much of a drinker, but even I downed glass after glass with gusto. Halkara drank a lot, too.

"It's fine if you drink, Halkara, but don't get completely plastered like you did at the wedding."

"When there's fruit liquor around, I always end up drinking it to compare the flavor, since I make plant-based drinks myself."

That's an elf apothecary for you. Plants are elves' specialty.

Just then, I had a eureka moment.

"Say, Halkara? Can you make several types of drinks that aren't alcoholic?"

"Yes. They don't have to be fruit-based, either. I can offer a healthier mushroom extract as well."

Then we'd be able to do this.

"On the day before the festival, let's host the Witch's House Café!"

My family's eyes all turned to me.

"What do you think? Halkara can be in charge of the drink menu, and the food Laika makes is good enough to serve at a restaurant. If we set up tables in the wooden shared space in the addition Laika built, we could use it as a venue without much trouble, and with our big family of five, we can serve the customers. And it'll be the day before, so it won't coincide with the festival itself."

No sooner had I proposed it than I pointed out plus after plus in an attempt to persuade the others.

However, one face didn't look particularly enthusiastic.

Oddly enough, it was Laika's.

"I see... In that case, we'll need to wear waitress uniforms, won't we?"

Oh, the ones that looked vaguely like maid outfits? I thought regular clothes would be fine, as long as we seemed put together. Actually, Laika's everyday clothes were pretty stylish already.

"Ordinary clothes would do, and if you'd rather not bus tables, you could work in the back. There's also the option of not doing anything at all."

It was wrong to force something like this.

"No, do let me participate, please! I also think it would be a good opportunity for your daughters to study society!"

Laika was sounding like a teacher. At heart, she was as dedicated as always.

"I'll put up with the waitress uniform... If we're busy, I expect it will stop bothering me before long."

Still, what does she have against waitress uniforms? I'd have understood if she was embarrassed, but Laika's style of choice was black Gothic Lolita. At this point, it already stood out more than your average outfit.

Well, if you're picky about fashion, you probably have inflexible standards.

The upshot was that we decided to join the celebration as a family on the day before the festival.

After we finished eating, when we went to report this to the village chief, he thanked us profusely: "That would be splendid!" From his reaction, you'd think we'd donated about a hundred million gold to the village.

The next day...

In the spirit of striking while the iron was hot, we went to the shop where we'd had our dresses tailored for the wedding.

We had waitress uniforms made for our whole group, and they completed the order for all of us without incident.

Since we had the opportunity, once we were home, we tried on our completed outfits together.

Mine made me seem like a perfectly ordinary server girl.

I felt like a high schooler at one of the maid cafés they often held at school cultural festivals in Japan.

I was a regular person who was wearing this on a whim, and a maid café professional probably would have told me I was doing it all wrong... If there even were any of those in this world.

Next, let's review the others.

First, Falfa and Shalsha.

"Does it look good on me, Mommy?"

"It fits comfortably."

They were a pair of splendid twin child maids. Marvelous. Truly marvelous. However, I was a little afraid to have them serve male customers like that. They were too cute, and I didn't want anyone looking at them in improper ways. After all, they were cute. Adorable, really.

Next, Halkara finished changing and emerged from her room.

"Um, they did take my measurements, but the chest on this is tight..."

Come to think of it, the shop clerk had said something along the lines of, "If it's a little tight, this one will make more of an impact."

It came as no surprise, but she was the busty elf waitress.

"When you're here, Halkara, things immediately get risqué. Conversely, I'm honestly impressed that you alone are enough to make this endeavor risqué at all."

"Madam Teacher, was that a compliment?"

"I think there's demand. However, if we only get a certain demographic, we'll have trouble... Listen, would you try walking around a little?"

"Just walk? You mean like this?"

Halkara walked.

Her bosom swayed assertively.

Wow, that swaying was enough to up the age rating. You almost had to wonder if her bust was made of water.

Even women would give that a second glance. We were absolutely going to get customers who were there for Halkara.

The last one to enter was Laika, who initially wasn't into this, and—

"Um, I... I don't look strange, do I?"

The moment I saw Laika, a shock ran through me.

Involuntarily, I covered my mouth with a hand and even crouched down a little.

"Hmm? Lady Azusa? Is something the matter? Are you feeling unwell?"

"It's a goddess... A goddess has appeared..."

I wasn't the only one who was reacting abnormally.

Halkara was also stunned. "It's the ultimate waitress..."

Yes, the waitress uniform suited Laika far too well.

It made her seem like an adorable girl who was serving customers for the first time and decided to try it on; her uneasy expression and the outfit's trimmings all harmonized with one another and her coquettish appeal. She was a force to be reckoned with.

"You wear frilly clothes all the time, so it looks good on you. Too good, actually..."

Laika was clearly embarrassed about this compliment.

"The truth is, long ago, I was a waitress in a play at dragon school, and everyone told me that it suited me… You're reacting the same way."

I see: She hadn't been enthusiastic because she knew it was almost too perfect for her.

"Laika, it may be embarrassing, but you really should do it at least once. Be more proactive about displaying your talents."

I was talking like I was a producer and she was an entertainer, but it was what I really and truly felt.

I had a hunch that we were going to be a success.

Well, all we'd done was have our clothes made, but the food would be relatively easy to deal with.

If we bought tables, they'd just get in the way later, so I was planning to borrow extras from the village.

And so we moved forward with the preparations for the Witch's House Café.

First, we came up with the menu. For drinks, we would offer the standards and rely on Halkara's instincts for the rest.

"Finally, I have the chance to give my abilities free rein! Just leave it to me, Madam Teacher!"

She seemed abnormally fired up, and she did submit lots of ideas for menu items.

However, despite the abundance of proposals, most of them were peculiar.

"'Drinkable Potency Enhancer—A Blend of Fifteen Different Roots.' This one's a no-go."

"Huh?! Why?! It was hugely popular with the men in my home province of Hrant. They said it worked wonders!"

"The concept is sketchy! Make it a bit more poetic."

"Well then, what about this? 'Drink It Daily and You'll Be Taller in a Month! An Herbal Medicine Blend that Promotes Bone Growth.'"

"Look, stop advertising how useful things are! Go with something more normal!"

Not only that, but it would be weird to sell an item with a one-month effect at a one-day-only café.

"I do think my suggestions sound witchier..."

Halkara's objection did make sense, but the people of the village didn't really fear me as a scary witch, so we didn't need to play the part too seriously.

"In that case, I'll play it safe and go with fruit juice. If you blend wild grapes in this region with honey dissolved in hot water, it has a refreshing aftertaste."

"Bring me ideas like that to begin with."

I could pick that one up without any complaints. As a matter of fact, there was nothing wrong with it.

"Well, I mean, it's just not interesting."

"Don't try for 'interesting.' These aren't gag products."

This wasn't an area where maid cafés were locked in fierce competition with one another, so "normal" would work just fine.

"If that's what you want, I can think of about fifty in a day."

"What are you, a genius? In that case, we'll be fine for drinks. Not that I was very worried to begin with."

"Drat... I'd at least like to make something like 'You Think It's Sweet, and Then Wham! Super-Spicy! Juice Blended with Thirty Spices.'"

No matter what world you were in, you could always find people who just wanted to do something weird.

Next was the food menu. That was also rougher going than I'd expected.

Laika brought in a plate supporting a huge yellow mass.

"Lady Azusa, I thought of a promotion in which anyone who eats this ultra-gargantuan omelet within thirty minutes will not be charged for it. What do you think?"

"No competitive eating gimmicks! We'll end up with a specific image!"

Are eating challenges a universal thing?

"Actually, I have one more secret plan!"

Laika went to the kitchen and brought out another plate.

"How about something unique? We'll put sweet cream on boiled pasta. People assume that pasta doesn't go with sweet things, and yet we'll top it with something dessert-like."

"I admire your adventurous spirit, but we're not doing that!"

They definitely had places like that in Japan, too!

"Laika, your regular cooking is delicious, so be truer to the basics!"

"I see… It's just that, we'll be taking their money and all, so I thought we really should provide them with commensurate value…"

Every one of them was far too adventurous. Café items should relieve and soothe people. I'd rather they didn't get that wrong.

However, there were worse troublemakers.

The door flew open with a bang, and Falfa ran up. She'd apparently been outside.

"Mommy! I caught a big grasshopper!"

She was right. It was a whopper, about the size of her palm.

"Wow, that is big."

"Listen, if we cooked this grasshopper, what do you think it would taste—?"

"We are not serving that at the café."

That was when Shalsha came up, holding a thick book.

"According to this volume, some foreign countries eat insects, and species related to grasshoppers are especially popular. However, unless you strip off the legs, they tend to catch in your throat or elsewhere inside your body, and you can end up in critical condition."

"I have no intention of denying other cultures, but we're not doing that here!"

Why would we want to take a one-day-only café in that direction?!

"You too, Falfa. Take Mister Grasshopper back outside, all right? He might have been planning to play with his friends."

"Okaaay. I will."

Falfa went outside again. Everyone was trying to do much stranger things than I'd imagined.

All right, I'll be the coordinator. There's nobody else.

The first thing I did was take care of seating. I used a tape measure and decided where we'd put the tables.

In addition to the indoor tables, I decided to set up outdoor terrace seating. That would give us more chairs, and the air was wonderful up there in the highlands. The occasional breeze felt pleasant, too.

I did this because if things got crowded, the atmosphere wouldn't be restful anymore, and that would mean our café had gotten its priorities backward.

I made the final decisions on the menu as well, taking Laika's proposals into consideration as I worked. I focused on dishes made with vegetables, settling on a slightly fancier version of home cooking.

"Let's write the menus on the sturdy paper we use to record medicine compounding results. We'll make one for each table. I'll handle the sample, so would the rest of you make three each?"

"Madam Teacher, you really are serious about this, aren't you?"

Halkara was so startled she'd drawn back a bit.

"I thought it would be more like a joke…"

"Why would we intentionally make a joke out of it when we're going to all this trouble?"

"No, I just meant, for example, we could say 'Welcome, Master' to customers and things like that."

Could Japan's maid cafés possibly be a universal thing…?

Time passed quickly—or rather, there wasn't much time until the day before the festival anyway—and the grand opening of the Witch's House Café arrived at last.

After breakfast, we all changed into our waitress uniforms.

"Y-you know, when we're all lined up in similar outfits, we make quite a sight..."

As Laika spoke, her expression was half-embarrassed and half-elated that the day was finally here.

I felt just about the same way.

"You're right. Fortunately, it doesn't seem to be raining today. Let's begin making the final preparations, shall we? Laika and Halkara, you start the food and drinks; Falfa and Shalsha, you wipe down the tables and check to make sure there's no dust on the floor. I'll put out the terrace seating."

If we'd set up the terrace seats ahead of time and it had rained, we would have had trouble, so we'd kept them under the eaves until right beforehand.

Everyone nodded, so apparently, there were no problems.

"It's just eight o'clock now, so we have two hours left before we open at ten. Let's do this right."

This time, Laika and Falfa responded: "Yes!" "Okaaaay!"

"Um, what will we do if we don't get any customers...?" Unsurprisingly, given how often we ended up in miserable situations, Halkara was a pessimist. "We are rather far from the village here. There are bound to be pre-festival celebrations there as well, and if they decide they don't care about a shop in a location like ours and give it a miss..."

She was right. It was a genuine risk.

"Well, there's no sense in getting uneasy. Let's just do what we can. I mean, you know, just participating is worth something..."

"If we don't move any product at all, I'll pack the drinks in baskets and go sell them at the festival tomorrow."

As you'd expect from someone who used to run a factory, she had a hardy commercial spirit.

"All right, let's get to work. You all know what your shifts are, don't you? Okay then, meeting adjourned!"

Since my work was outside, I went to open the door in the side of the gabled log cabin. This was technically the back door of the house, but since we were using the cabin as the shop, it would be the front entrance.

There was a standing signboard in front of the house that read, THE WITCH'S HOUSE CAFÉ. That said, almost no one ever passed by here, so it would really be a question of how well word had spread through the village beforehand.

"Now then, I'd better get the outside tables set up neatly, too—"

However, the moment I opened the door, I froze.

There was already a looooooooooooooooooooooooooooooong line of customers outside.

It had to be sixty people or so… We certainly didn't have that many seats.

About half were men, and half were women. Just looking at them, you would have thought they were about to hold a convention.

"Ooh! The great Witch of the Highlands, waitress version!"

"What a glorious sight!"

"I want to hurry and see the others, too!"

All I'd done was step outside, and a great cheer went up.

"U-um, you do know that we don't open until ten, don't you?"

I was pretty sure I'd attached a paper with our business hours on the sign in front of the shop, but…

"Of course!"

"Staying here all night would have caused trouble for people, so I came very early in the morning!"

"We took a full day to come here from the town!"

The person at the very back held a placard with END OF THE LINE written on it.

I don't remember making that! Did some volunteer do that on their own?

"We're getting ready right now, so wait just a little longer, please!"

I never dreamed that I'd have this many eyes on me as I set out the tables. That said, thanks in part to my tremendous physical strength, the work itself was over quickly. It was easy to carry a table in each hand when you were level 99.

However, I couldn't tell them to wait almost two more hours until we opened at ten.

I finished the outdoor preparations fast, then went back inside.

"Listen, there are already about sixty people lined up out there. Do you think we could open a little earlier, at nine?"

Everyone looked startled.

"What?! It's rude to line up the night before!"

Apparently, in this world, standing in line all night was considered a nuisance. The exhibition-and-sale culture in Japan was similar. *Why are they similar?*

"Actually, it sounds like they lined up starting early this morning."

"That's all right, then. If they'd been there all night, we would have had to send them to the back of the line."

They had pretty strict rules regarding the overnight crew.

"So do you think we'll be able to open at nine?"

"The drinks won't be a problem. What about you, Laika?"

"I'll make it in time as well. We already have the ingredients. However, we do have more customers than we'd anticipated, and it would be a problem if we sold out, so perhaps I should fly to the village now and arrange to have additional groceries delivered."

"I'll do that. Just tell me what you need! Then it's down to the number of chairs, I think…"

We did have spare tables on hand. Maybe I'd go grab what we had in our rooms. We'd use those to expand when we had to field large numbers of customers.

Right then, before I said anything, Falfa and Shalsha carried in a table.

"Mommy, Shalsha says we should put out more tables."

"Mom, I'll do what I can, too. An eastern scholar said that learning which does not lead to action is meaningless."

"You two are fantastic! If we had time, I'd hug you again!"

And so we worked like mad to make our nine o'clock opening.

It might have been the first time that I'd worked this hard in this world.

Still, it held none of the exhaustion of being enslaved to a company.

Maybe that was only natural. Wage slaves work because they're forced to.

Right now, we were working because we wanted to. Our motivation was fundamentally different.

Then the second the hands of the clock pointed to nine, I flung open the log cabin door.

"Since we have so many customers waiting, the Witch's House Café is opening an hour ahead of schedule! We'll help you starting from the front of the line, so please be patient!"

A cheer rang out: "Yeaaaaaaaaah!" *Nobody yells like that for café openings!*

I had no idea we'd be this popular...

The line was even longer than it was earlier. No question, we were going to be working all day.

"That's one party of two! Would you prefer to sit inside or out on the terrace? All right, follow me inside!"

"Party of one, correct? Would you be all right with sitting at the counter? Yes, come this way!"

"Party of five! Follow me to this table, please!"

I fielded customers right and left. As I worked, I remembered to smile.

Oh, and that "counter" I mentioned was a long table that we'd hastily shoved against the wall. Our original plans hadn't included anything like that.

The idea of having people relax and take it easy was already disintegrating. If we didn't raise our turnover rate significantly, some customers weren't going to get in at all. And here I'd been dreaming of a secret café hideaway...

Still, the customers had been aware from the time they joined the line that things would be crowded, and we didn't get any complaints. In fact, people cheered as if we were idol singers until it became a problem. Well, not a problem so much as embarrassing...

"You're a beautiful waitress, great Witch! Simply divine!"

"Halkara is exquisite, too! She's right on the line between 'wholesome' and 'lewd'!"

"The twin waitresses just couldn't be cuter!"

Hmm... My hole-in-the-wall restaurant was rapidly turning into a maid café.

As an aside, about half the customers were women. Japanese idol singers have quite a few female fans, too; this was probably something similar.

However, no matter what, the most popular—the one who attracted the most attention—was...

...Laika.

"Thank you for waiting... Here is the omelet you ordered. Do take your time and enjoy it, please..."

As a rule, Laika was in the kitchen, but every once in a while, she'd bring out an order herself. Every time she did, the customers' eyes went to her.

If the customers were eating, their fork or knife hands stopped dead.

"Sh-she's an angel..."

"You mean 'a goddess.'"

"If I had a little sister like that, I'd spend an hour every day hugging her, I just know it."

"There's no need for all these words. Just gazing at her is sublime."

Laika was perfectly adorable here, too. She'd captured the attention not just of the men but of the women as well. A table of teenage girls was squealing.

As a matter of fact, she'd overwhelmed me, too, the first time I saw her. This proved my senses hadn't been mistaken.

If there were a ranking for beautiful girls you'd want to have as your little sister, she'd take first place easily... Although a little sister in a waitress uniform might be a bit odd.

"Um, honored guests, if you stare at me like that, I, um... It's very hard to relax..."

Laika was blushing and fidgeting, and it made her even more formidable.

One customer had gotten worked up enough to get a nosebleed.

"Laika really is the one, isn't she?"

"It's great when earnest girls wear something like that."

"Halkara's good, too, but she's too provocative."

"After all, there's more to feminine appeal than boobs."

"I mean, I do like boobs, too!"

I'd started to hear slightly problematic comments here and there.

Should we just keep this up and start earning money as a maid café? No... I'd rather have a life of steadily killing slimes.

Not everything was going as we'd planned, but the café itself was very popular.

"This juice is really refreshing!"

"Yes, and the soup warms you right up. It feels like home cooking, but it's sophisticated enough for a café as well!"

Everything on the menu was high quality. I was confident that people would be satisfied, and it was all thanks to Laika and Halkara. Although, if I hadn't kept an eye on things, we could easily have had a lineup of outrageous items.

However, being popular meant we were busy, and so...

Before noon, Shalsha was sitting down in the back.

"Mom, my legs won't move anymore. I'm sorry."

It was true that Shalsha wasn't very strong physically. This work might have been hard for her.

"Take your time and rest. I'm sorry I was too busy to notice earlier."

"I-in that case... I'll be the cashier. I can do that without moving around."

"All right. When you think you can't handle any more, though, speak up right away. Don't tough it out."

If we were flustered, it was in a good way, but even so, I hadn't expected this much business. There were a lot of faces I didn't really recognize. Apparently, people had come not just from Flatta but from farther away.

If this had been a ramen shop in Japan, we probably would have been able to say that we'd run out of soup and needed to close for the day, but we were a café, and since we were only open for this one day, we couldn't exactly tell people to come back some other time.

Guess I'll just have to pick up the pace.

A table opened up, so I had to let in the next customers. I opened the door with a bit of a flourish.

"Thank you for waiting! How many are in your party?"

"One."

I saw a very familiar face.

"We do seem to run into each other a lot, don't we, Beelzebub? Is your work with the demons that slow?"

"You're being rude to your customer. I've got a good ear for such information, nothing more."

Beelzebub was the sort of high-ranking demon who frightens crying children into silence, but to be honest, she was a good person. In the past, she'd really saved me.

"However, as far as I can tell, the success of your business is giving you some trouble."

"So you can tell, huh? Honestly, it's so busy I'd take help from a cat..."

Just then, I hit on a brilliant idea.

Well, actually, it was more of a plain old request.

"Hey, Beelzebub, if you don't mind, do you think you could help us serve customers?"

I clapped my hands together and begged. Petitioning a demon this way felt a bit like heathen worship.

"Hell's bells… You always instantly opt for using me as a handyman. I am a demon, I'll have you know. I'm not a being you can just casually put to work. One can only be so impertinent. —Sure, I'll help."

"Thank you so much!"

To be blunt, I'd thought things would work out if I asked Beelzebub. That was the type of person she was.

"If you bow to me like that, I really must reward you."

Beelzebub spoke a little bashfully.

"By the way, do you have a waitress uniform? I could work in what I'm wearing, but if I'm doing this, I'd prefer something frilly like that."

She was really into this. Maybe she'd wanted to try wearing the outfit? That said, Beelzebub's everyday clothes exposed her shoulders, and it was true that they weren't really suitable for a daytime café.

"I do have a spare uniform, just in case this one gets dirty. Go ahead and wear that."

"Right. I'll find an empty room and change."

Help me out, Beelzebub. I'll pay you proper wages! If you end up working overtime, I'll pay extra!

After I waited a few minutes, Beelzebub called, "Okay, it's safe," and I went into the room.

Beelzebub stood there, looking as stylish as one should in a waitress uniform. Hmm, yes.

"The size was perfect. This isn't half bad."

She was inspecting her outfit in the full-length mirror. She really was enjoying herself.

However, one thing felt odd to me.

"Oh… Your wings are poking through the clothes. I'm only borrowing the spare outfit, and now it has holes in it!"

"Oh, you can repair holes like these with a Mending spell."

"Huh? I didn't know there was such a convenient spell. I've never heard of it before."

"If you don't know it, then I suppose it's only handed down among the demons."

The demons might have stumbled upon a serious advancement. Although that spell would put repairmen out of business…

Beelzebub briskly rolled up her sleeves.

"All right. What would you like me to do first? I'll show you the customer service technique of a high-ranking demon!"

"Um, let's see… Could you go take orders? There's a little piece of paper with a number stuck to each table, so you'll be able to tell what the table numbers are."

"Leave it to me. I'll do the work of ten."

Gallantly, Beelzebub charged into battle (figuratively speaking, I want to stress).

Now that a new staff member had appeared, the customers' eyes focused on her.

"Th-there's a newcomer!"

"She's more refined than any of the other staff members so far!"

"No, I'd say her aura is closer to a military dignity!"

True, Beelzebub was a high-ranking demon, and even the way she walked was impressive.

Her movements were completely economical, and her back was ramrod straight.

However, there was one thing that worried me.

Beelzebub was generally overbearing. Was she even capable of serving customers? She wouldn't address them as "Hey, you," would she? I heard there was a place like that in Akihabara, but our concept was different.

Beelzebub efficiently loaded up a tray with glasses of water, then marched over to a table of customers who'd just been admitted to the café.

The customers braced themselves a little. *Here comes a weirdly arrogant-looking server*, they were probably thinking. The child was actually scared.

However, that was when the unexpected happened.

Beelzebub's face shifted into a very smiley, friendly expression.

"Welcome! ♪ Here's some water for you! Thank you for visiting the Witch's House today! Once you've decided on your orders, just let me know!"

Magnificent service! Even though she can't have actually practiced for any of this!

On top of that, when customers ordered dessert sets, she actively made suggestions: "I believe this tea would pair well with that." She had the technique of a veteran waitress.

"All right, I have your order! Wait just a moment! Thank you very much for your visit today!"

The youngest customer actually began expressing approval. "You're pretty, lady!"

"Thank you. When you grow up, you'll be dashing, too. All right, I'll be back! I'll bring your food shortly, so wait just a moment!"

Am I dreaming...?

I'd anxiously assumed that she'd say, *I'm important. Order something simple that won't cause me trouble, then hurry up and leave.* Apparently, my fears had been unfounded.

Not only that, she didn't even sound condescending like she usually did.

"Kitchen, one herbal tea and carrot chiffon cake set, plus two mixed fruit juices!"

"A-all right..."

In the kitchen, Halkara was nervous.

Later on, I got an opportunity to talk with Beelzebub.

"What do you think? I work like a fly, do I not?"

That expression didn't exist in the human world, so I didn't know what she meant.

"When you're working as a server, you even talk differently."

"I only act arrogant when my position engenders the expectation of superiority. Where's the sense in a waitress acting more important than the customers? I'm not such a fool that I don't know how these things work."

She was absolutely right, and I had no complaints.

"Whoops, I had an order for fruit crepes to call in. Maybe I'll draw a picture on 'em with chocolate sauce."

"You can do things like that, too?!"

"There is nothing I can't do," Beelzebub said, clearly proud of herself.

After that, Beelzebub did tricks right and left, filling teacups from incredible heights and drawing pictures in the foam layers on our drinks.

"Lady Azusa, we've acquired an astonishing helper…"

Laika was watching Beelzebub pour tea from a teapot held high above a cup.

"I knew it. When you're in trouble, you should ask for help. You mustn't just bottle these things up inside."

Beelzebub had said she'd do the work of ten, and she hadn't been exaggerating one bit.

Thanks to that, customer satisfaction at the Witch's House Café soared even higher.

"One herbal tea! Got it. Thank you very much!"

I heard Beelzebub's cheerful voice again.

When I thought about it logically, we were probably the first café in recorded history to have a high-ranking demon serving people as if that were normal.

With Beelzebub's help, we finally managed to get some breathing room as we ran the Witch's House Café, and somehow we made it all the way to closing time at seven in the evening.

The whole staff assembled to see the last customers off.

""Thank you for visiting us today!""

Then, after it was all over, I threw my arms around Beelzebub.

"Thank you! You really and truly saved us!"

"Yes, I'm well aware that you're grateful to me. You may praise me more."

Right then, I'd have liked her to look as triumphant as she wanted. She'd earned it.

"Yes, I will, I'll praise you!"

"In that case, as a sign of your gratitude, let me order something off your menu. After all, I originally came here as a customer."

She was right. I'd made a customer work all this time. If you thought about it, we were one lousy café…

"Oh, of course, that's fine. Order as much as you like. Naturally, it's all on the house."

"Well, let's see. In that case, I want everything on this page of your food menu, plus this cake, this one and this one, these three drinks, and also this."

"You're eating too much."

"I just did a mountain of work, and I'm hungry. Bring me two bottles of Nutri-Spirits, too."

That wasn't on the menu, but Halkara went to get them right away. She acted like she was dealing with a scary older alum from her school.

Laika and I got the food ready. In the meantime, Beelzebub and my daughters had a nice chat.

"Here, Falfa. It's a book about differentials and integrals."

"Yaaaay! Thank you, Beelzebub!"

"And here's a book on demon history for you, Shalsha."

"Thank you. I'll read it very carefully."

In Japan, there were aunts who really doted on their nieces, and maybe this was something similar. Beelzebub was very indulgent with Falfa and Shalsha. Actually, she listened to a lot of my requests, too, so it was possible she was just indulgent with everyone.

However, maybe because my daughters were exhausted from a level of work they weren't used to, they fell asleep with their books open.

I would have felt mean if they'd woken up while we were carrying them to bed, so I covered them with a light terry-cloth blanket instead.

Then we set Beelzebub's enormous order in front of her.

We put out plates for our own meal, too. After all, we hadn't had enough time to really eat.

"Mm, yes, this is good enough to sell. It's rather unsophisticated here and there, but there's no point in offering court cuisine at a café, and I expect it's fine as it is."

Guess that counts as a passing grade.

"Originally, I heard they were holding a festival in a village near here, and I came to see it. Then they told me you'd be running a café the day before, so I decided to stop by and laugh at you."

"I see. And then I put you straight to work. I'm sorry."

"It looked as if you'd break down before long if you went on like that. The villagers probably got excited at something so extraordinary and turned up by the dozen."

"I think that's about the size of it. We got roughly four times as many customers as we were expecting."

When Halkara had totaled up the sales a little while ago, we'd made quadruple the estimated amount.

I'd had Halkara do the cashiering because she seemed likely to know the most about it.

As an aside, Beelzebub ate silently while we talked. She was a pretty healthy demon.

"All right. I did have one other reason for coming here."

Beelzebub brought out a paper with something written on it in the demon tongue.

"I can't read Demon at all... And that's one wordy letter...," I replied.

"I'll summarize it. It says: 'Azusa, the Witch of the Highlands, has been selected as a recipient of the Demon Medal. Her presence is requested, should her schedule allow it."

"Oh, right, the Demon Medal, sure. —Wait, what's that?!"

I'd never heard the word before.

"I'm not even a demon! I may be a three-hundred-year-old immortal, but I'm human!"

"Ah, the Demon Medal is not a medal awarded *to* demons, it's a medal awarded *by* demons. It matters not who or what you are."

I see. Even Japan sometimes gave awards to people from other countries.

"You are in the peace category for resolving the dragons' dispute, see. What impressed them was how you obtained a de facto promise of lasting peace instead of merely routing the enemy. Well, I'm the one who recommended you, but anyway."

I take my eyes off her for one minute, and this is what she does!

Also, the demons appreciated my work for peace? They were wreaking havoc on their image.

"It won't happen for a little while yet, but you should all take advantage of this wonderful chance to visit the demon kingdom. I'll give you such a fine welcome it'll make your heads spin."

"In that case, we'll go. We owe you for several things, and I'd feel bad saying no."

"Mm-hmm. Very good."

However, Laika had a cautious personality, and her worry was written all over her face.

"Um, is it safe for us to go to the demon country? It would be wonderful if everyone was like you, Beelzebub, but…"

"These days, almost nobody wants to go to war with humans, so there's no need to fret."

From the way Beelzebub spoke, it didn't sound like there was anything to be concerned about. It would probably make for a good change of pace.

"All right. Lady Azusa has a tendency to get pulled into trouble, so I am a little worried, but…"

"Huh?! Why are you criticizing me, Laika?!"

Laika's going through a rebellious phase!

"It isn't criticism. I trust you, Lady Azusa, naturally. It's just that you really do tend to get pulled into trouble. Facts are facts."

When someone tells you something so bluntly, it's hard to argue…

"And blundering is a way of life for one of us."

The glance she sent Halkara's way was a little chilly.

"What?! The trouble's spread to me now!"

"Halkara, behave so that you don't anger the demons. Unlike Lady Azusa, you aren't able to protect yourself, so do be careful."

It sounded as though Laika was the parental figure here.

"I'll be okay. I'm used to traveling. The first time I went to a different province, my travel funds were stolen during the journey, but I worked a part-time job and got back home just fine."

"What, you were robbed?!"

I retorted without thinking.

"No, no, it wasn't much money at all. The next time I went on a long journey, I ended up surrounded by a group of rather alarming individuals, but some soldiers on guard duty saved me, no problem."

Laika looked at me and said, "You see? We should worry."

"You're right… When the time comes, I'll keep an eye out. Particularly for Halkara."

Sometimes people operated on the assumption that being safe once meant they'd be safe again. Halkara was clearly that type.

We let Beelzebub stay the night. After she'd helped us out so much, we had a duty to show her thorough hospitality.

"I'll get the bath ready, and you can go in first. If you like, I'll even rinse your back for you."

"In that case, I'd like to bathe with Falfa and Shalsha."

"They're asleep, but… Well, I guess they should take a bath before going to bed. All right. I'll wake them up."

At that, Beelzebub seemed incredibly happy.

She looked ready to ask me to let her adopt one of them again. She was welcome to dote on them, but I wasn't giving her my daughters.

"I brought these for the two of them."

Beelzebub revealed a few hollow toy ducks.

"You float them in the water. It makes bathing more fun."

"So they've got those in this world, too…"

My daughters were happy to take a bath with Beelzebub, so it worked out.

Even after Beelzebub got out of the bath, she seemed to be having the time of her life as she toweled my daughters' hair.

"Aaaaah, I swear, they're both so darn cute!"

She really does love kids, doesn't she?

"They're so cute, I'd love to take one home with me!"

"I knew you were going to say that! That's absolutely not going to happen, all right?!"

She seemed liable to actually do it, so I told her N-O straight out.

After her bath, Beelzebub discussed Nutri-Spirits and other things with Halkara.

"I wonder if we could grow any extra-nutritious plants in the demon lands. As the minister of agriculture, I'm promoting policies to expand our number of commercial crops."

"Hmm. In that case, could you send me data on the regional climate? I'll make up a list of things that might grow there based on that."

When it came to things like this, Halkara was a pro. She might be scatterbrained, but she really was an expert as well.

We whiled away the evening, and before we knew it, it was time for bed.

"Well, why don't I go walk around the festival with you tomorrow?"

"Yes, that would be good, too. Let's do that."

And so the long day at the Witch's House Café came to an end.

The next day, our little family—Beelzebub included—went to the Dance Festival in the village.

It was still morning, but already people were dancing all over town.

There were long rows of stalls selling everything imaginable, and I do mean everything. Some of them were even selling things people hadn't needed at home, the sort you'd see at a flea market in Japan.

"Oh-ho. For a country festival, they appear to be putting considerable effort into it."

"So today you're being condescending, are you? Although you are objectively correct about it being a country festival."

Compared with a metropolitan festival, naturally, this one could get only so big.

That was just fine. "Plain and simple" was perfect.

However, even if the festival was plain and simple, walking through it in company like this inevitably created a huge uproar...

"Ohh! It's the great Witch and her entourage!"

"That talented waitress from yesterday is here, too!"

"Go on, clear the way!"

The crowd smoothly parted in front of us, as if we were Moses.

"No, no, no! Just act normally, please! You're making me self-conscious, so it's actually harder to walk!"

However, once the villagers got like this, they wouldn't budge.

"No, no, we insist! Please, you should walk down a wide road!"

"He's right! You're rather like gods, anyway!"

Of course this would happen...

"There's no help for it, Lady Azusa. I believe it would be all right if you behaved like a god, just for today."

You're flattering me, but you aren't much different, Laika the dragon.

"In that case, you try walking as if you think you're a god, Laika. I'll follow you."

"I—I don't want to... I could never do something so outrageous..."

"There, you see? You shouldn't insist that other people do things you wouldn't do yourself."

But this time, we had one person who was used to acting arrogant.

"Oh-ho. I see the villagers around here know their place."

Beelzebub strode boldly down the Moses road, radiating self-importance.

Falfa copied her, marching with her chest thrown out. Shalsha followed, hiding behind her sister.

Well, as long as things stayed rather charming like this, maybe it was all right.

We bought and snacked on foods from all sorts of stalls, occasionally throwing ourselves into the dance.

Chicken, mutton, pork, beef—there were quite a few grilled skewers on offer. After all, skewers were something you could eat while you walked around.

"Laika, which kind do you think is best?"

"Let's see. The mutton interests me; they seem to have seasoned it with a spice blend."

"Why not just eat all of them?"

Beelzebub had bought every kind, as if that was normal.

"You're the type who's never even considered dieting, aren't you?"

She was an indulgent carnivore, in the literal sense of the word.

"I never gain weight, no matter what I eat."

That comment was at the top of the list of statements that irritated women.

"Besides, I'm always busy working."

We seemed to run into Beelzebub an awful lot, if that was the case. Was she really working?

"Hmm? Come to think of it, I haven't seen Halkara in a while…"

After a quick look around, I spotted her lying on the ground, dead drunk.

"Ooooooh, I can't drink any more…"

"Argh, honestly! Would you quit sleeping on the ground?! Learn your lesson already!"

There was no help for it, so I pulled her up.

"At the very least, *I've* learned, Lady Azusa."

Laika took out a small bottle.

"What's that?"

"It's a drink Halkara developed. It works on drunkenness, or so I'm told. By the way, it's so incredibly bitter and astringent that you'd never believe it was of this world. I made sure I had some on hand." Laika poured it into Halkara's mouth. "This is sure to wake her up. That's how powerful it is."

When the drink had been in Halkara's mouth for about half a minute—

"Bleeeh! What is this?! It tastes like someone poured concentrated anguish from the depths of Hell down my throat!"

"What on earth does it actually taste like?!"

"Who made this slop?!"

"You did! You made it!"

"Oh, the sober-up drink? That tasted so bad it didn't sell..."

Halkara was in her right mind again immediately. Whew. Good, very good.

We'd walked around the center of the village quite a bit, so we rested at a café.

Technically, the place was a house that was ordinarily used for a completely different trade, and it was acting as a café only for the duration of the festival. In other words, it was doing the same thing we'd done yesterday.

There weren't many shops in the village, so they had to bolster their numbers this way during the festival.

People came from the neighboring towns as well, which meant the population density was double what it usually was.

"Shalsha, this festival actually originated far away, you know," Beelzebub was commenting.

"I heard a festival celebrating a fertility goddess spread all the way here. It's very intriguing."

"So you knew, did you?"

Beelzebub and Shalsha were talking about something academic, but as long as you were basically having fun at festivals, you were doing it right. Even now, merry dance music was playing outside.

"Actually, not too long ago, the days of festivals like this one were used to encourage encounters between men and women. People would meet at the festival, then spend a passionate night together."

"Hey, no, hold it! Don't fill my daughters' head with strange ideas!" *It's still too early for that!*

"This is merely a scholarly conversation. Besides, there's nothing wrong with men and women falling in love."

"Augh... I understand your logic, but..."

That was when Shalsha sniped Beelzebub like the most trained assassin.

"Say, Beelzebub, have you ever loved a man?"

"Wha—! What are you saying, Shalsha...?"

"Well, the conversation just drifted that way. Neither Shalsha nor Falfa know much about it."

"Argh... I am rather unfamiliar with the topic, myself. It's not my specialty."

Beelzebub had flushed a very deep red.

Oh. She was the type who could talk about sex in general but had no idea what to do when she was the subject of the conversation.

Actually, if this is what she's like, she can't be used to romance.

"Falfa wants to hear, too!"

Then Falfa joined the fray. Beelzebub was completely cornered.

"I-it really is too soon for you two. Rather, I don't think it's appropriate for me to be the one to explain it... Ah, of course! You should ask your mother about it."

"Aaah! You just passed the buck!"

"Shut up! You didn't want to be talked about, remember?!"

When I looked to the side, hoping someone would throw me a bone, Laika was obviously feigning ignorance. She'd put up a barrier that would keep her from getting pulled into this conversation.

Laika did seem earnest. She probably wouldn't be a fan of love-related jokes, either. Maybe I should leave her alone.

Halkara would probably just say "Liquor is my lover" or something, so I'd skip her—

"Madam Teacher! You just thought it would be pointless to ask me about anything romantic, didn't you?!"

Erk. She was onto me.

"You know, people I've never met before often make advances at me, but they get disillusioned once they see me passed out drunk."

"So liquor really *is* your lover."

As we discussed these irrelevant topics, the village chief entered the shop.

"Great Witch, I hear your café did outstanding business yesterday!"

"Yes, thank you. We were so busy it was kind of a problem."

The village chief had also paid a visit to the shop with his wife, just so you know.

The chief's position didn't allow him to neglect the Witch of the Highlands. I heard that getting along with me was even included in his official duties.

"On that note, if you wouldn't mind, we were thinking we'd like to have you ride on the gondola."

He made a proposal I didn't really understand.

"A gondola? I've ridden on a dragon before, but…"

"This is more like a box with wheels."

Oh, like a Japanese festival float.

"It weaves through the festival at its climax, and many people have told us that they'd love it if you and your companions rode it. The men who weren't able to go to the café yesterday practically begged!"

"Haaa. It's embarrassing, but an opportunity like this doesn't come around often. If all you need us to do is ride on it, I suppose we could."

"If possible, we'd like you to wear your waitress uniforms. The villagers would be thrilled…"

What's with that request?

Laika was already blushing. "Again…?"

Still, riding in our ordinary clothes and watching people be disappointed would be unpleasant in its own right.

I thumped Laika's shoulders.

"Let's help them out, Laika. It is a festival, and we'll call this a special bonus."

"A-all right… If you say so, Lady Azusa…"

And so we rode on the gondola…

…as waitresses.

To put it bluntly, the crowd completely lost it.

"Long live the great Witch!" "Long live the great Witch!" "Long live the great Witch!!!" "Thank you so much!"

All we were doing was waving from a moving gondola, but the cheering was tremendous.

I felt as if I'd been reborn as a wildly popular idol singer. It was a bit embarrassing, but if it was making people happy, I'd deal with it.

"Lady Laika!" "Lady Laika, you're fantastic!" "I also went to the café yesterday!"

Hmm? People were cheering pretty loudly for Laika, too…

"E-excuse me! Please don't call me 'lady'! Plain 'Laika' is fine!"

Come to think of it, they actually were calling her "Lady Laika." Even though they'd mostly just called her "Laika" at the café…

"The way she's blushing is just perfect!" "Be my little sister!" "Lady Laika!"

Wow… Had our café completely awakened the villagers to Laika's cuteness? I might have inadvertently done something pretty mean to her…

"My, Laika, aren't you lucky! You're incredibly popular."

Halkara's remark was no help at all.

"I'm not terribly good with this sort of…"

Laika, if you act timid, it's gonna backfire and you'll probably end up making yourself look more adorable. Still, I wanted to see her like that for a while longer, so I opted not to say anything.

My little sister is far too cute!

"Waaah, Lady Azusa, make yourself more visible! Please, take the attention off me!"

Unable to stand those fervent gazes, Laika began to beg. She physically clung to me, if I had to be specific. True, if the looks were all, I could ward them off, but the audience was getting incredibly worked up: "Ohh, you know, this is good, too!" "So noble!"

"Aaaaah, my cute little sister is clinging to me. I'm so happy."

"Lady Azusa, what are you saying?!"

The gondola that carried our group of waitresses became the festival's most popular event.

After that, the village chief asked us to do it again next year, since they could count on attracting visitors that way.

"I'll take Laika's attitude into consideration before making that decision."

"Great Witch, please make it a regular event!"

I see. This is how festivals become an established annual custom.

That was what I thought as I listened to the villagers enthusiastically pleading for repeat performances.

AZUSA AIZAWA

The protagonist. Commonly known as "the Witch of the Highlands." A girl (?) who was reincarnated as an immortal witch with the appearance of a seventeen year old. Before she knew what was happening, she'd become the strongest being in the world. Although she's had some rough times, it has ultimately given her a family, and she's delighted about it.

PERSE-VERANCE EQUALS POWER. I ONLY DO THINGS I CAN STICK WITH!

LAIKA

A dragon girl and Azusa's apprentice. She's fastidious and cares a lot about what others think, but she's a good, earnest, hardworking girl. Gothic Lolita clothes, maid outfits, and other frilly things suit her very well (which embarrasses her).

LADY AZUSA, I'LL DEVOTE MYSELF TO IMPROVING AGAIN TODAY!

"Excuse me, Madam Teacher. Could I trade my meal duty on the day after tomorrow for your shift today?"

Halkara asked me on the morning of the fifth day after the festival had ended and peace had returned.

"That's fine, but is something happening in two days?"

"I'm going to Nascúte."

Nascúte was the town next to the village of Flatta, about an hour's walk away. I went there occasionally, but only occasionally.

It was too far to go for shopping, and it wasn't an incredibly large town, so there weren't many goods unique to the place.

It wasn't very interesting; my only impression of it was that it was like a slightly bigger Flatta.

That said, since it really wasn't far, it would have been weirder if it was unique.

"Why are you going to a place like that?"

"A preliminary inspection. All right, I'm off to water the flowers."

And with that, Halkara was out of her chair and out the door.

That made it hard to ask what the inspection was preliminary to…

The next day, during a lunch break, Halkara was flipping through some papers in the dining room.

"Let's see…," I heard her say. "I'd want to have about this much space. Actually, I think I might prefer something a bit larger. Still, I guess I'll just have to negotiate directly with the realtor."

Hmm? A realtor? Was she purchasing land or a building?

Could it be...?

Was Halkara planning to buy a house and live on her own?!

As a matter of fact, I'd suspected something like this might happen. All this time, I'd messed with Halkara and treated her as a comic relief character. Halkara herself was the one who'd created the root cause, but even so, she probably hadn't enjoyed my joking around.

I could declare with utmost confidence that when it came to her skills as an apothecary, I wasn't treating her as anything less than full-fledged. However...she was lax about her personal life and other things, and as a result, I might seem to be finding fault with her quite a lot...

What should I do? Should I ask her not to leave?

She hadn't said a word to me about going, though. Under the circumstances, would it be odd to try to persuade her to stay?

Besides, she was an adult, free to choose what to do with her own future. This wasn't like telling your college-age child to commute to school from home.

While I was worrying to myself about that, Halkara went off somewhere.

"Calm down, calm down... You don't know for sure that that's what's going on yet."

Thinking I might have made some sort of mistake, I looked at the papers Halkara had left.

Every last one of them was real estate information from Nascúte.

Not only that, but there were red check marks on them.

"Argh! This looks serious!"

Just then, Laika came up. She seemed a little flustered.

She was also sending furtive glances this way and that, keeping an eye on her surroundings.

"Um, Lady Azusa, could I have a moment?"

"Sure. What is it?"

"I'm not certain yet, but do you think Halkara intends to leave this house?"

"You thought so, too, Laika?!"

I didn't think we should have this conversation right there, so we took it to my room.

"The other day, she was in the room where she makes medicines and said, 'At the next place, I'll be able to take up more space.' I wondered if that 'next place' might not mean a new home."

"You're right… She really is planning to leave…"

She was already a working apothecary; I hadn't had much I could teach her. Had I done anything teacher-like? I really doubted it.

"I did some research on Nascúte. Its altitude is lower than ours, which means that the forests near the town are deep, and it's likely she'll be able to gather a variety of medicinal herbs there. I wonder if that isn't why she plans to move…"

For a little while, Laika and I were silent.

"Should we ask her not to go?"

I didn't know what to do, so I asked Laika.

"I think it would be fine either way. I believe that's a decision you must make on your own, Lady Azusa. However—ultimately, the right to decide lies with Halkara. I do think we've lived like family, but after all, we aren't a real one."

She was right. Not only that, but Halkara hadn't spoken about it with either of us directly.

In other words, she wasn't even torn. To a certain extent, she'd made up her mind.

"Yes, Laika, thank you. I've found my answer."

I gave a rather wistful smile.

"And what is your answer?"

"Stay here for a minute. I'm going to call my daughters."

I came back with Falfa and Shalsha, who had been reading difficult books in their room.

"First of all, you mustn't tell Halkara what I'm going to tell you, no matter what. Is that clear?"

"Uh-huh!" "Yes."

My daughters agreed.

I told them that Halkara was probably planning to leave this house.

"What?! Big Sister Halkara is going away?!"

Falfa looked like she might cry.

"Falfa, shh. Unfortunately, it's very likely."

"I did think that might be the case," Shalsha interjected. "I heard Halkara say, 'It is about time I made a fresh start.'"

Ah, as I thought. Well then, we'll just devote ourselves to doing what we can.

"Listen, this is a decision Halkara's making for the sake of her own happiness, so I don't think we should get in the way. That said, even if she does leave this place, we can make some good memories, can't we?"

Falfa nodded vigorously.

"So tomorrow night, let's throw a big surprise going-away party for her!"

"I'm just wondering, but why tomorrow night?"

An excellent question, Laika.

"Because the day after that, Halkara is going to a realtor in town. If our scheme manages to touch her heart, she may decide to stay here after all."

In other words, it was both a going-away party and our last chance to keep Halkara here.

"We'll hold a farewell party, but I don't want to say good-bye. That's what I really think."

Practically speaking, we had a little more than a day. We needed to get ready at top speed.

"Laika, you take care of the party food, please."

"Yes, I will. By the way, what sort of dishes do you suppose Halkara likes?"

"She likes liquor more than food… I think she does like vegetables. Maybe it's because she's an elf."

"You're right. I'll make things as vegetable rich as possible."

"And I'll fly over and buy some luxury liquor."

If we didn't use money now, when would we use it? I'd fly to Vitamei, the capital city of Nanterre province, and buy Halkara liquor so expensive it'd make her uncomfortable.

"Mommy, what should Falfa and Shalsha do?"

Let's see… For my daughters… Right. I'll have them make full use of their privilege as children.

"You two write a message card."

"What's that?"

"Write a letter, then read it in front of Halkara. 'We've had a lot of fun living with you, Halkara, and the memories, etcetera, etcetera.'"

That should be pretty effective. She might start to consider staying after all.

"Um, and also? Shalsha is pretty good at drawing portraits."

The big sister had just delivered some shocking news.

"What, really? I had no idea…"

"She's embarrassed to show her pictures to people, so she keeps them hidden. She hasn't drawn lately, either, so you probably wouldn't know, Mommy."

Shalsha seemed uncomfortable that Falfa was talking about her. Her eyebrows had turned down to form an inverted V.

"I—I'll show them to people once I've gotten good. Until then, I'm sealing them away."

I wanted to see them very, very badly. My daughter drew those pictures. Of course I wanted to see them.

"Hey, Shalsha? If you don't mind, would you let me look at them?

I'd really love to see your pictures. I don't know anything about this side of you, and I want to."

"All right. But don't say that they're good even if they aren't. Inaccurate perceptions cloud eyes that would otherwise see the truth."

"All right. I promise. I won't mislead you, Shalsha."

Shalsha nodded, then said, "I'll get them," and ran out of the room. "They're like this…"

When she returned, she timorously held out something that looked like a sketchbook.

They weren't colored, but they were insanely good.

Several of them were photo-realistic portraits, probably of people Shalsha had met in town. Some of them seemed to be of Shalsha herself.

"So this isn't like when a mother goes, 'Oh, wow, you're so talented,' just to praise a child. You really are good at this. And that's not all, either; you can sense something like the subject's spirit in these. The idea that this person is probably nice is clearly expressed."

Laika had leaned in to look at the pictures, and she sounded astonished as she offered her opinion. "You could apprentice yourself to a painter with these. You really should develop this talent."

"They're not good enough to show people yet, so this is embarrassing…"

If these weren't good enough to show, I'd like her to tell me what dimension they'd have to be in before she could do that.

I placed my hands on Shalsha's shoulders.

"Shalsha, I'm putting you in charge of drawing Halkara's portrait. It can be a little rough—just draw it. Even if she does leave, I think she'll probably treasure it her whole life."

"All right, Mom. I'll do as you ask." Shalsha nodded. "Promise you won't come to look at it until it's done, though. It's more embarrassing to have people see works in progress."

"I won't look. I promise. I won't pull a *Grateful Crane*."

"*Grateful Crane*?"

"It's a children's story. A crane who'd been saved from a trap turned herself into a human and came to repay the favor. She worked on a loom, but she'd told people not to look, and they did anyway. Then they saw that she'd turned into a crane to do the work, and she left."

"Oh, that's similar to the Kalshurah folktale from the south."

That was a humanities-type remark, and I didn't really understand it. She probably meant there was another story like mine out there, though.

In general, we'd settled on the preparations we were going to make, and I went to buy the drinks before the day was out.

I bought one bottle of wine for three hundred thousand gold and one bottle of distilled liquor for five hundred thousand.

I wasn't even going to think about how many slimes that was. I had that much in savings. As a matter of fact, I could have bought ten bottles if I felt so inclined.

Then dawn broke, and the day of the party came.

We still had a problem, though: If Halkara was in the house the whole time, we wouldn't be able to get ready.

"Halkara, I want to go mushroom hunting after lunch. Would you come help me?"

"Oh yes, Madam Teacher!"

Perfect. Operation Get Halkara Out of the House was a success.

We ate lunch, then left for the forest. I'd been to these woods many times before Halkara came here, but I'd learned the names of several of the mushrooms there from her.

"We're a little late today. We usually do this in the morning."

"I have my reasons."

The thought that this might be the last time we worked together made me feel a little disconnected.

"Madam Teacher, you look lonely. Did something happen?"

"I suppose you could say I was thinking about good-byes."

"Oh, is it the anniversary of your beloved's death or something similar?"

Halkara had gotten the wrong idea. Still, she wasn't too far off.

"Even if death isn't what's separating you, sometimes you find out you'll have to say farewell quite suddenly, you know?"

"Yes, you're right. The one saying good-bye worries about when to bring it up, too."

Oh! That sure is telling...

"I've lived a rather extraordinary life, but I always want to keep my good-byes clean. I suppose you'd say I want them to be meaningful for both parties. Where you can take the next step forward, without dragging regrets behind you."

"...Yes, you're right."

"Um, Madam Teacher, are you crying?"

"N-no, I'm not."

The evening was growing later. They were probably ready by now.

"Halkara, shall we go home?"

"Yes, Madam Teacher!"

She might call me that only a few more times.

When we reached the house, I said, "Wait outside for a moment," then went in to tell everyone we were back.

Then I returned to the entryway.

"Sorry to keep you waiting. All right, come on in."

"Of course... What happened?"

Mystified, Halkara entered the house and opened the door to the dining room.

""Halkara, thank you so much for everything!""

Everyone smiled and spoke in unison.

The ones with free hands were clapping.

"Um, what is this? You've put up a sign that says, 'Halkara, please continue to do your best'..."

Halkara didn't know where to look in her confusion. Our surprise was a success.

Great, let's take the operation to the second stage.

Falfa came to stand in front of Halkara.

"I'm going to read you a letter."

"Huh? A letter?!"

"Dear Big Sister Halkara. You made Falfa lots of yummy juices. You also told me lots of stories about interesting plants, and now looking at mushrooms is so much fun for me. You're a little scatterbrained sometimes, but you absolutely never got mad at anybody, and you were always nice. Knowing that you're moving away makes Falfa very sad. If possible, I'd like you to stay here and tell me all sorts of other stories, but I also want you to do more things in a new place... It's probably going to be hard sometimes, but... Please don't give up, and keep smili— Ngh, waaah... I don't want you to gooooo..."

Overcome with emotion, Falfa began to cry.

It felt odd to tell my crying daughter "Nice one!" but I was sure Halkara's heart wasn't immune to that.

"This is for you!"

"Oh... Th-thank you..."

Halkara took the letter.

"Um, what in the world is...?"

Then it was Shalsha's turn.

"I drew this with you in mind, Halkara."

It was a picture of Halkara sitting in her compounding room. As always, it was phenomenal. You could even tell what Halkara did for a living.

"Um, I... Thank you very much."

Halkara was bewildered, but she accepted the picture as well.

"All right, enough gloomy talk. Today, let's drink and be merry!"

I set the liquor on the table.

"It's a three-hundred-thousand-gold wine, Tears of the Goddess, and a five-hundred-thousand-gold distilled liquor called Opulence! I splurged like you wouldn't believe, so be sure to savor them properly before you get drunk!"

"Whaaaaaaaat?! Madam Teacher, is this some kind of mistake...?"

"It's not a mistake! You're planning to move to Nascúte, aren't you?! Today we're celebrating the start of your new journey!"

For some reason, Halkara had rapidly gone pale.

"What is it? You think you're going to cry, too? It's all right—go ahead. After all, there's no one but family here, and we'll be family even if we're apart!"

"You've clearly got it all wrong! I don't intend to move!"

Halkara's scream echoed through the room.

We all stared blankly at her.

"Huh? But you're going to the realtor in Nascúte tomorrow, aren't you?"

"I'm going, but I don't plan to move."

"Then why? Do you mean you'll only move out if you find a good house?"

Was it like waiting to turn in your resignation until after you'd been given an informal offer from a potential new employer?

"No, listen to me, I don't even want to leave! I'm going to the realtor to set up a medicine and beverage factory in Nascúte!"

Come to think of it, she'd mentioned ages ago that she was thinking about a factory…

"Huh? …Wait, so this was all a misunderstanding on our part?"

"I suppose that's what it would be. At the very least, I'm planning to continue living at this house."

In other words, this was no longer a going-away party.

"Oh. I guess I shouldn't have worried, then."

My shoulders slumped. All my energy was gone.

"I blew eight hundred thousand gold, just on the beverages."

"I'm sorry, Lady Azusa. I should have gathered more evidence…"

"Excuse me, but isn't everyone sort of acting like I'm in the wrong?! That can't be right, can it?!"

However, the children were as purehearted as one might expect at a time like this.

"So you aren't leaving! Falfa's happy!"

Falfa clung to Halkara.

"Oh, thank you! It feels like somebody's finally happy about this!"

She was right. This was definitely cause for celebration, so all we had to do was turn this into another sort of party.

"In that case, starting now, we'll begin the Congratulations on Not Going Away, Halkara party! Everyone get some alcohol or juice for the toast!"

That day, we dined in extravagance.

"Aaaah, this wine is truly mellow and full-bodied. I just can't get enough."

"Of course it is. Weep as you drink it. I've almost never drunk anything with a price tag like this."

About the only times would have been when I was invited to village functions and they'd opened expensive bottles for me.

"The food is incredibly good, too. Did you focus on things I would like?"

"I kept your preferences in mind as I cooked. Personally, I would have gone for a few more meat dishes, but in any case, it won't do to have leftovers, so please eat up."

Laika brought out dish after dish.

None of the individual plates seemed all that big, but she'd apparently decided to compete with quantity.

According to Halkara, Nascúte was near enough that she could get there and back on foot, and as the company president, once things were on track, she wouldn't have to go in every day.

"By the way, doesn't it take vast sums of money to set up a factory?"

"I'm investing my earnings. However, it's designed so that I won't be in debt even if it fails, so that part's safe. Since I'm doing this in completely new territory, there are many potential liabilities, so..."

When it came to administration, Halkara seemed reliable, so I supposed she would be all right. Besides, she had a track record of success.

"The town of Nascúte is in the foothills of the mountains. That means the groundwater flows right to it, so it's rich in spring water. If

I use that water, I'll be able to sell large quantities of Nutri-Spirits and other health drinks!"

So she really had thought that part through.

"Besides, there would be a limit to labor in Flatta, but in Nascúte, I should be able to hire a staff of ten or so. If I put the citizens of Nascúte to work, I'll be creating jobs, too, so I don't think it's a bad deal for anybody."

"I see. Work as if you're planning to turn it into the town's specialty."

"I will! I'll work like mad!"

Three minutes later, Halkara had drunk herself under the table and was unable to make productive conversation, but...

"I expect it will go well," Laika said with a smile, as if she was watching over her.

"You're right. Once the factory opens, maybe we should throw another party."

We'd managed to congratulate a family member on the start of her new venture at any rate, so let's call that a happy ending.

Halkara's project moved forward on schedule until finally it was almost time for operations to begin.

Even though this was a factory, it didn't have a host of gigantic pipes running through it or a production line manned by the latest robots. This wasn't that sort of civilization. At its heart, it was no different from an ordinary shop.

It felt like a slightly expanded version of home manufacturing, and they pasted the labels onto the bottles by hand.

As far as the construction of the factory itself was concerned, Laika had called in some dragon acquaintances and had them help out, so in a mere five days, the work was just about finished.

Halkara had said, "I have construction funds left over, so I'll reimburse you for that expensive liquor from the farewell party...," but she didn't need to worry about that.

Just treat me when you start turning a profit.

That said, they'd completed only the building, and the factory wasn't operational yet. For a little while, Halkara was extremely busy making arrangements for the equipment and systems to bring in the necessary materials; she worked from early in the morning until almost midnight and completely wore herself out.

Laika, in her dragon form, took her to and from work.

It would have been pretty dangerous to have Halkara and her wayward body out on the road at night.

"Um, don't you think you're working too much? Whatever you do, don't work yourself to death..."

"No, no, even if I'm tired, I can keep up the fight a while longer if I drink a bottle of Nutri-Spirits. It's just that, lately, I've been going through more bottles per day..."

That was clearly a bad sign! I couldn't stand by and not interfere just because she was an adult!

"Starting now, make sure you're home by eight in the evening! That's an order from your teacher!"

"Umm... If I do that, the work will be delayed..."

"Then hire people and figure something out! If you push yourself and try to handle everything on your own, you really will collapse! Collapsing isn't even the worst that could happen; what if it kills you?!"

"Madam Teacher, you just won't compromise on that, will you...?"

Halkara's eyes were wide in the face of my vehemence.

"Well, I've died of overwork once myself..."

In my previous life in Japan, I'd just keeled over one day. When I told her about the regret I'd felt, Halkara's expression turned appropriately grave.

"I understand. I'll ensure that my staff members can balance their work and home lives! I'll take proper days off as well!"

And so, having half forced Halkara to improve her abysmal labor conditions, I thought the factory would begin operating without incident. However...

"I just can't seem to get a staff together."

Even though it was morning, Halkara was wearing the expression of an elf at a wake.

"Why not? Are your wages that low?"

"Of course not! On the contrary, what I'm offering is clearly higher than average over there."

In that case, there must have been some other reason.

Were people steering clear because the profession was unique? Maybe people were more conservative there, since the area was rural.

"It keeps popping up. Apparently, the place is famous for it."

"Popping up? You mean spring water?"

"No, we'd be in trouble if we didn't have that. I mean a **GHOST**..."

Halkara intentionally said the words in a creepy voice.

"A ghost, huh? Do things like that really exist?"

Frankly, I wasn't convinced.

"I thought they must be pulling my leg as well. However, yesterday, I saw it, too. I was working at night when a girl with bobbed hair who seemed to be about fifteen..."

And so Halkara explained...

Several hundred years ago, a merchant who'd gone bankrupt had apparently lived on that land. The merchant had tried to get money by selling his fifteen-year-old daughter to a red-light district, the story went. Up until immediately beforehand, the daughter had apparently been told that she was being married off to a wealthy nobleman and was giddy with excitement. But when the day came, she found out about her fate. They said she succumbed to her despondency and hung herself.

As a result, even after a different building was erected on that site, the ghost of the girl apparently haunted it and caused disruptions.

That was an awful lot of *apparently*s and hearsay, but it was nearly impossible to get clear information regarding stories like that, so there was no help for it.

The tale was notorious in the town of Nascúte, and the mere idea of working in a place like that was enough to keep people away.

"I thought it was odd that the land was so terribly cheap..."

"So they fobbed off a troublesome piece of property on you, hmm?"

She might be a talented administrator, but Halkara tended to be careless about things like this.

"In other words, if that ghost disappears, everything will work out just fine! I want to do something about it!"

"In theory, that's what would happen, yes."

"So, Madam Teacher, would you help me?"

"Huh?"

My reply sounded pretty reluctant.

"I'm...not good with things like that. You know, situations where you might get cursed..."

I just had no immunity to scary stories. Things about hexes, say, or cursed villages.

"But you're a witch! You'd be fine! Besides, when someone's as strong as you are, Madam Teacher, even a ghost will run away! Exorcise it, please!"

She says that like it's so easy...

I didn't have any exorcism-related spells. Wasn't that a job for the clergy?

Maybe I should ask someone who knows about this stuff.

...And so I asked Shalsha, who'd studied the humanities extensively.

"In academic parlance, ghosts are called 'disembodied anima.' It's the general term for souls that have left their physical bodies."

"That's too technical and hard to understand. Break it down a bit for me."

"Disembodied anima fall into two categories. One type is tied to the spot where it died and is very nearly incapable of movement."

That would be a type of location-bound ghost, then.

"The other is relatively free to move and can fly anywhere it wants to. In this case, all sightings have occurred in the place where it died, so I assume it belongs in the first category."

"In other words, it's a location-bound ghost. Is there a way to deal with it?"

"It would be possible to use a cleric's item and expel it by force, but unless it shows clear hostility toward humans, clerics won't do things like that. The act is said to desecrate the soul."

That meant we'd just have to handle it ourselves...

I went back to Halkara and told her what Shalsha had said.

"All right. Let's go over at night and take a look."

"Thank you so much, Madam Teacher!"

"—But only if a helper comes with us."

"A helper?"

"I'm calling Beelzebub."

Since she was a high-ranking demon, there was no way she'd be scared of ghosts.

I'd already been taught the spell for summoning her.

Actually, she'd told me there was a spell to call her and had taught it to me when we first met. I hadn't used it before, but she had dropped by of her own accord when we'd opened the café, and I figured she probably wanted me to invite her to things anyway.

Earlier, Laika had observed, "Since she's a very important person, I would imagine it's difficult for her to make friends with other demons. She has authority as well, so people may try to ingratiate themselves to her, but it's probably hard to find genuine friends." That might be pretty accurate.

As a result, I didn't hesitate to call Beelzebub. I went outside, drew a magic circle, and performed a special chant.

"*Vosanosanonnjishidow veiani enlira!*"

The words sounded enigmatic because they were in Demon, and the ancient version of the language at that.

I didn't really know what it meant, but with chants, you only need to get the pronunciation right anyway.

An ominous, blackish miasma rose from the magic circle, which meant it probably worked.

Thinking that this spell felt about as witchy as you could get, I waited for a response.

And waited.

Patiently.

Five minutes passed.

Well, it's not as if this is the door owned by a certain cat-shaped robot. I guess she won't show up immediately…

"I'll go back to the house for a bit."

When I went inside, I found Beelzebub. For some reason, she was soaking wet from head to toe.

I thought I'd probably bungled things somehow, so I softly closed the door.

It promptly opened again.

"Hey. You summoned me. Why are you avoiding me?"

"I just… I thought maybe I'd made some sort of mistake…"

"Indeed you did! Thanks to that, I met a terrible fate! Your pronunciation was sloppy and summoned me to the wrong place!"

I see. So that demon spell summoned her directly.

"And why was your bathtub full of lukewarm water at this time of the morning?! It was a calamity and a half, being dropped in there!"

"We keep the previous day's leftover bathwater and use it to water the field. Pretty green of us, huh?"

"Be as green as you like, but don't summon me into it!"

The words to that chant had been in ancient Demon, so pronouncing them was never going to be easy. There were several different types of inflections, too.

By the way, Beelzebub was fluent in our language; Demon was a completely different language, and it was also pretty difficult to write.

"I'm sorry. I'll practice more next time."

"Hell's bells… Still, it's strange that a human was able to use a demon spell at all after only being taught once. You really must have a prodigious talent for it…"

Was that my level 99 advantage?

Halkara hastily prepared a drink for Beelzebub. Apparently, she hadn't thought Beelzebub would be here so soon, either.

"And? What did you want?"

Beelzebub was soaked and in a bad mood. This was the worst possible time to be asking for favors.

"Halkara will tell you about that."

"What?! Madam Teacher! Please don't put me on the spot!"

This is your problem, actually, so throw me a bone.

"I won't get angry, so say what you want to say."

"In that case, I'll tell you. I'm setting up a factory in a nearby town, but…it's haunted, and I'm having trouble, so… Um, we…we thought that, if the demon Beelzebub was there, the ghost might get scared, and maybe things would work out somehow…"

"You went to the trouble of summoning me for such a petty trifle?!"

"You said you wouldn't get angry! It's not fair to get angry now!"

On that point, Halkara was correct. However, parents always promise not to get mad if you tell them the truth and then get mad anyway, don't they? My parents used to split hairs and explain that they weren't getting mad, they were just scolding me.

"Argh, for the love of… You summoned me right out of a meeting about agricultural promotion, and over a thing like this… The bureaucrats are surely going to read me the riot act later."

Not only that, but apparently, we'd called her in the middle of a pretty important meeting.

"Well, I'm here now, and there's no help for that. Show me to this factory. I'll thrash your ghost for you."

If it was the ghost of a little girl, I'd rather she didn't actually do any thrashing.

"Um, ghosts only come out at night. Do you think you could wait until then, please?"

"In that case, would you at least wait until evening to call me?!" Beelzebub exploded again.

"I'm sorry. It's just that no one told me I'd be summoning you directly."

"That's true… It's all my fault… Let me borrow an empty room until it's dark. In the meantime, I'll draw up something to share at the conference that nobody will be able to complain about."

We waited quietly for night to fall.

As an aside, Beelzebub lamented, "If night had come a little later, I would have finished the materials..." Apparently, she'd worked the whole time.

Like Flatta, there wasn't much foot traffic in Nascúte at night, and it was quiet.

Actually, maybe the towns of Japan had been abnormally bright. Naturally, nothing like neon signs existed in this world.

Night was when people slept. It was a mistake to work during times like that. That's why I was against overtime. When the sun sets, stop working! ...Drat. More memories from my former life...

The factory was so hushed that it was creepy.

"Listen, Azusa. You've been alive for three hundred years yourself, which makes you practically a monster. What do you need me here for?"

"I'm bad with ghosts and that sort of thing. If it doesn't have a physical body, I can't defeat it."

"But Falfa and Shalsha are made from the collective souls of slimes... Well, there may not be any logic to things like this."

Beelzebub strode inside.

I knew I'd chosen the right person for the job.

Since nothing in this world ran on electricity, deserted buildings were perfectly silent at night.

If we'd at least had the sound of a refrigerator or a ventilator fan, I probably could have relaxed a bit, but...

Since we didn't have the courage to press forward through pitch darkness, we'd brought hand lanterns.

Come to think of it, I was pretty sure there was a spell that illuminated dark rooms. Maybe I'd study that one.

"Ngh, it feels like this place is haunted..."

"Are you an idiot? Isn't this haunting why you called me? We can't defeat the ghost if nothing shows up."

Quite the pragmatist, this demon.

"Listen, Beelzebub, can I hold your hand?"

"Hold my hand...? Hmm, hrrn... Do as you like. It is embarrassing how it makes me feel like a young lass, but...it's not as if I'll lose anything by it."

As she spoke, Beelzebub reached back with her right hand. She really was a reliable older-sister type.

"Madam Teacher, hold my hand, too, please!"

Halkara took my right hand. As a result, all three of us ended up holding hands as we advanced, which looked pretty strange.

Walking side by side would have made it hard to maneuver, so we angled our bodies sideways as we advanced deeper into the building.

"Linking up like this has made us a lot heavier. It feels as if we've turned into a human centipede demon—a demon with several bodies joined together. The first time they see it, most people are terrified."

"N-no scary stories!"

"Yeah, yeah, all right. Even if this puny ghost shows itself, it won't beat me, so you don't need to worry."

I couldn't really tell, since I was staring at the floor, but Beelzebub seemed to be looking around as she walked.

"By the way, Halkara. Where does this thing manifest?"

"It appeared when I was working in the room just up ahead..."

"I see, I see. In that case, we'll focus our investigation there."

"Um, that place scares me, so could we please not do that?"

"Would you two quit it already?! You summoned me to look into this, so why are you trying to call it off?!"

Logically, Beelzebub was entirely correct, but there was nothing rational about things like this... I wished she wouldn't blame Halkara.

"We'll go look in that innermost room."

"N-no, don't! Let's at least save it for last! Please! Please!"

"Halkara might have a point. Why don't we play word games here until we've got the audience warmed up, and then go?"

"Both of you are morons. And do you honestly think word games would warm up an audience? That's what groups of girls do when they can't find anything to talk about."

In the lead, Beelzebub charged ahead like a berserker.

At this rate, it might have been okay to just let Beelzebub handle the whole matter alone, but at this point, we were just as scared to turn back without her, so there was nothing we could do.

Then we stepped into the notorious haunted room.

Just as we did, for some reason, the lantern flames winked out.

"EEEEEEEEEEEEEEEEK!!!!!"

"Yeeeeeeek!!!! Madam Teacher, please save meeeeee!"

Halkara and I both screamed at the same time.

"Shut up, would you?! You two are more of a nuisance than the ghost!" Beelzebub yelled, adding another voice to the mix. "Oh. But there's a ghost, too," she added casually.

"AAAAAAAAAAAAAAAAAAAAAAAAAAAAAAAAAAAA AH!!!!! There's a ghooooooooooooooost!!!"

"Eeeeeeeeeeeeeeeeeeeeeeeeeeeeeeeee!!!!!!!!!!!! I'm gonna wet myself or worse! I can't hold it iiiiiiiiiiin!!!!"

"You're far too noisy! Cool your heads a bit, would you?! It's just a ghost! The soul of a dead woman! What's scary about that?!"

"No, that's the scary part! Hey, why are you fine with it?!"

Possibly because she was irritated, Beelzebub shook off my hand. *Don't! It's much scarier now!*

"I'll wager you're frightened because you can't see her. In that case, I'll do something about that for you. Sit tight."

"Huh? What are you going to do? Is there some spell that will get rid of terror?"

"No."

There was no such convenient spell.

"Hey, spirit woman! Show yourself! You can manage that at least, can't you?! You've stayed here all this time, so I won't let you say you can't! Hey! Girl! Answer me!"

Beelzebub started yelling at the darkness.

"I am Beelzebub, a high-ranking demon. I'm the demon kingdom's minister of agriculture and as such, I possess the authority to make your grave a site for dumping horse manure!! I'll dump horse manure on every last place where you have fond memories!!"

That was blatant, horrendous harassment!

"On top of that, inflicting damage on a spirit is a walk in the park for a demon of the upper echelons. You shall suffer more than you did when you died! Are you okay with that? Show yourself before I count down from ten, or I'll slaughter you!"

She's threatening to slaughter a ghost!

"Ten, nine, three, two, one, zero!"

And she just skipped a bunch of numbers! She didn't even count all the way from ten!

At that, a table-esque piece of furniture in the room began to clatter.

"Eeeeeeek! The ghost is angry!"

"Oh-ho, so the table's moving, hmm? So what? What's so scary about a moving table? If the table moves, does it put me at some sort of disadvantage? Tell me that, ghost!"

Beelzebub's voice sounded menacing.

"If you have something you wish to say, then come out. No matter what sort of past you had, if you willfully frighten people who come here, then you're no different from a pest. I'll exterminate you without a shred of hesitation."

Beelzebub was way too strong. I was so glad I'd brought her along.

It felt as though my own fear was rapidly fading, too.

Oh, and Halkara was clinging to me for dear life and trembling: "Gods, gods, I beg you, save me... I'll do anything, anything..." *Although we're depending on a demon right now, not on the gods.*

"What's this? Do you object? Would you like to try cursing me, then? It won't work. No mere spirit woman could curse a high-ranking demon. Would you rather I cursed you with magic instead?"

If anyone out there was troubled by ghosts, I highly recommended taking a high-ranking demon with you. Now that I was thinking about it calmly, it wasn't even possible for a ghost to be scarier than Beelzebub, was it?

"Oh? You intend to run? I won't let you! You won't escape!"

I guess the ghost is scared, too.

"Hold it right there!"

Beelzebub spread her wings and flapped up toward the ceiling. It was dark and I couldn't see clearly, but that was what I could make out.

"What is it?! Are you fighting?!"

"No! I'm slaughtering her, that's all!"

What a fiendish thing to say! Oh wait... She is a fiend.

"All right, puny spirit, now you'll pay for making a fool of me."

How odd. For some reason, I was starting to want to cheer on the ghost. That poor spirit...

"Um, I'd rather you didn't do anything that's going to get us cursed..."

"Never fear! Curses happen because the ghost exists. If I destroy it, the entity doing the cursing will vanish, so no harm will befall you, either!"

Argh! This really does seem like murder!

"Okay, I've caught her! Light the lanterns!"

Halkara and I both did as we'd been told.

"Aaah! There's something there!"

There was a new person at Beelzebub's side.

Well, I wasn't certain whether it was accurate to call her "a person." All I knew for sure was that the individual was a girl of about fifteen or sixteen, on the verge of tears.

"Sp-spare me... I didn't think a devil like her would show up..."

The girl spoke in a quivering voice.

"Madam Teacher, for some reason, I seem to be seeing something I shouldn't be able to see..." Halkara sounded dazed. "Do you suppose I drank too much and am beginning to hallucinate...?"

So she's aware that she drinks enough to worry about that?

"I can see her, too, so I don't think that's it."

"Did you drink too much as well, Madam Teacher?"

Let's get away from blaming things on alcohol.

Beelzebub descended, still holding the ghost in a full nelson.

"Humans ordinarily can't see spirits, but the spirit can make itself visible. This one must have decided that seeking help from you two was the wisest move."

"Um, Beelzebub, do you mean to say that that individual is the ghost?"

Even though we could see her now, Halkara was hiding behind me.

"If you want details, ask her."

Something felt odd about asking a ghost if she was a ghost, but we weren't likely to get anywhere if we didn't.

For now, we had the apparition sit down on a chair.

From time to time, when the light struck her a certain way, she looked translucent, but that was probably because of her spiritual nature.

"What's your name?"

"Rosalie... I'm the ghost of the girl who offed herself in the house that used to be here."

She was terribly brusque.

Then she began to tell us about herself.

"They told me I'd be getting hitched to an aristocrat. In my town, I had a rep for being all sweet and ladylike, and I believed it could happen even if it did sound like a dream. But my damn old man and the damn old hag made up the whole damn thing..."

The poor girl. Even her parents had betrayed her.

"The men in town used to hit on me all the time... Would I have been happy if I'd just up and run off with somebody? Well, whatever. It's too late now anyway."

"We understand what happened, but I mean, were you really ladylike?"

The way she spoke was rough, and even now, she was sitting with her legs really wide apart.

"Once I was a ghost, over time I...went kinda rogue."

Apparently, it was a little embarrassing for her to say she'd turned rebellious, given the way she averted her face.

"You know, that sounds plausible. Being betrayed by her parents could change an adolescent girl to this extent," Beelzebub commented.

"This is my turf. I've protected it this whole time, thinking outsiders should make like outsiders and keep their distance... And then you people came."

That wrapped up her story, for the most part. We knew the ghost's identity now, and she'd surrendered, so the incident should have been pretty much resolved.

"So... Rosalie, wasn't it? What do you want to do now?"

"Huh? ...What do you mean, 'do'?"

We hadn't heard a thing about the girl's future yet. We'd heard only about her past.

"Oh, I'll erase her in the blink of an eye, so she won't suffer."

"Proposal rejected."

This helper had no qualms about saying some terribly mean things!

"Why? She feels pain and stays here because she has a soul. If I erase her existence, she'll be released from all suffering. If you return to nothingness, the pains of birth, sickness, old age, and death don't exist for you."

"I'd rather you didn't use force to make Buddhist ideas a reality."

"In that case, go to the church and have a cleric offer prayers for the repose of her soul. That should purify her, and she won't stay in this world any longer."

In other words, we'd be making her pass on properly. That did sound like the correct answer, but...

Rosalie hugged herself tightly.

"No…" The word sounded strangled. "I don't want to be snuffed out yet…"

Her voice was trembling a lot more than ours had when we'd been afraid of her ghost.

Well, sure. Of course she wouldn't want to disappear.

"It's not rational for ghosts to stay in this world to begin with. You make some rather selfish requests."

Beelzebub was too much of a pragmatist. It just wasn't that easy to come to terms with some things.

"Well then, Rosalie, why not stay here?" I offered, as if it was perfectly normal.

If she was afraid of disappearing, that was just about the only alternative.

"D-do you mean it…? I'm in the way, though, right?"

Rather than being happy, Rosalie answered with astonishment.

"Of course, if you're planning to wreak havoc, I'd say, 'No, hold it,' but you aren't doing any harm just by being here, are you? You don't cost anything in food, light and heating, or taxes. In that case, no harm no foul, right?"

"Hmm. No harm, huh? If the ghost maintains an appropriate attitude, I suppose it might turn out that way."

Beelzebub seemed to have no particular objections.

"What…? You mean the ghost would be here at my workplace?"

Halkara was obviously shaking. I supposed she hadn't yet conquered her fear.

In my case, those feelings had faded significantly as soon as I'd laid eyes on the ghost. Beelzebub's idea that things weren't scary once you saw them seemed to have been correct.

"Why not? If thieves got in at night, she might chase them off for you."

"That may be true, but… When I'm not sure if she's there or not, it's hard to relax."

"Why not have her stay solid all the time, then?"

"That would be weird, too! And! Besides! Merely having a ghost on the premises is making ordinary people reject this place and refuse to work here!"

"Oh. Now that you mention it, that's right."

A fun workplace environment, complete with ghost! Please come and join our team— No, that probably wouldn't fly. This was a factory, so if we didn't resolve the haunting issue, the place couldn't do business. Even if Halkara got used to the situation, it wouldn't solve the fundamental problem.

"I guess it's really not okay for me to be here... Ghosts are a pain in the butt, aren't we...?"

Even Rosalie was turning pessimistic. I wanted to tell her that that wasn't true, but it was a fact that she was hindering factory operations. We had to find a solution.

"Wait. Come to think of it, can't you go anywhere besides this factory?"

"Nope. I've never left the lot of the house where I killed myself."

As Shalsha had said, location-bound ghosts really couldn't go elsewhere.

"There is a way," Beelzebub said.

"Ugh, you're so right, there's really no good way, is there? —Wait, there is?!"

"There is. When it comes to soul research, demons are far ahead of you people. If the spirit can't leave this place on her own, we simply have to move her out of it. No need for any complicated measures."

If she couldn't move, we just had to carry her. As a theory, I understood it. The problem was how.

"Tell me! What do I have to do?!"

Rosalie seemed interested, too.

"The spirit has to possess a living person, then use that person to travel somewhere else. Once they've reached an appropriate spot, yank the spirit out. It's like moving house, using a human."

"Hmm. So she just has to possess somebody, huh?" I said. "I don't really want to be possessed, but..."

"Any spirit should be able to attempt possession. However, she is not the only one involved, and it's not as if a ghost can possess absolutely anybody. For example, it's near certain that it wouldn't work on you, Azusa."

Then Beelzebub's eyes went to Rosalie.

"I've never tried possessing anybody before…"

"Make like you're diving into the other person's head. Give it a try. Even if you fail, it won't kill you."

"All right. I'm ready. Go whenever you want to."

I closed my eyes and braced myself.

"A-all right, well, here goes nothing."

Spak!

There was a sound inside my head as though something had bounced off it, and then Rosalie was breathing raggedly in front of me.

"What was that? I'm beat… I haven't been this wiped out since I was alive."

"To make a long story short, people with exceptional abilities don't leave any openings for possession. People with absolute confidence in themselves are also tough. Unless the person is weak willed and easily swayed by others, possession is hard to manage. In other words—"

Beelzebub's eyes went to Halkara.

"Um… Why are you looking at me?"

"She should almost certainly be able to possess you."

"Wha— Huh?! Was that a stealth insult?!"

"I'm not being stealthy. You seem weak willed, and you are practically vulnerability incarnate."

"That's really too mean, in a variety of ways!"

Slowly, Rosalie closed in on Halkara.

"Sorry 'bout this, but help me out a sec."

"No! I'm no good with psychic phenomena! I won't be able to go to the bathroom when I wake up in the middle of the night!"

"So I'll possess you and walk you to the bathroom, then."

"That's what makes it so scary!"

Before Halkara was finished speaking, Rosalie dived into her head and winked out of sight.

Did that mean it had worked?

"Hey, I can move this thing."

The voice was Halkara's, but her tone was completely different. She was moving her hands awkwardly, like a robot.

By all appearances, Rosalie had gotten in.

"It worked! That's terrific!"

"I haven't had a body for a while, and it makes me feel antsy... Plus, this one's got an incredibly heavy chest."

Halkara (?) put her hands under her bosom and lifted it. Meaning she had enough of a bosom that this was possible.

"Yes, good. Now all you need to do is leave the factory and we're all set."

True, we'd be able to move Rosalie out of the factory, but we still had a problem.

"So where are we taking her?"

We hadn't even thought about that.

".......Your house. Where else? You were the one to suggest saving her. Take responsibility."

"You're right. Besides, we're chasing her out for our own convenience. And so—"

I held out a hand.

"Rosalie, would you like to live at my house?"

"C-can I? It won't cause you problems or anything?"

"You were unhappy until you died, so why not become happy now, after death?"

I'd learned too much about this girl to just abandon her.

Moving Halkara's hand clumsily, Rosalie shook mine.

"It's a deal, then. Let's get along with each other!"

As I shook Rosalie's hand, I gave her my very best smile.

After all, she had to be nervous, and she'd been all alone for an extremely long time. Emotionally, she should be handled very gently.

"Y-yeah… Thanks…" Rosalie expressed her gratitude, flushing red.

"I have lots of rooms at my house, and even a ghost should be able to have a nice life there. I haven't told any of the other residents yet, but they're all kind people, so it'll work out."

Then, for some reason, Beelzebub heaved a sigh that sounded like profound resignation.

"Azusa, you are a con woman. Not only that, but the fact that you hardly realize what you're doing makes it difficult to deal with."

"Huh? I don't really get it, but are you disgusted with me?"

"It may not sound like it, but I am praising you, in my own way. One can spot the calculations of a schemer, but you don't calculate anything. That's the most pernicious type."

If she's going to praise me, I wish she'd do it in a way that's easier to understand.

"U-um… You're Miss Azusa, right? Can I call you Big Sis?"

"As far as appearances go, I look like the older one, don't I? Sure. You can call me anything you like."

"I'll follow you forever, Big Sis. If something happens to you, I'll protect you with my life!"

"Protect me? But you're already dead."

I'd only taken it as a joke, but—

"Nah, if I borrow a body like this, I can use it!"

As she spoke, Rosalie puffed out her chest.

Since the chest was actually Halkara's, the gesture had considerable impact.

Now that we'd settled the matter, it was time to return to the house in the highlands.

Halkara couldn't fly. Consequently, Beelzebub went to call Laika so we could have her ride on the dragon's back. Once she'd explained the situation to Laika, Beelzebub immediately went to sleep in a guest room. *Thanks for all your hard work so late at night.*

After a short while, Laika arrived at the meeting spot outside the town.

"I'm Rosalie the ghost. You're Sis Laika, right? It's good to meet you!"

"Hearing that from Halkara's mouth feels very strange… The look in your eyes is different."

"I'm only in here for now. Once we're at the house, I'll get out."

It wasn't long at all before we were back. Laika's ability to fly was a huge help.

Falfa and Shalsha hadn't gone to sleep yet, so I introduced them to Rosalie.

"Thanks for helping me out like this! You're Big Sis's daughters, aren't you?"

"Uh-huh, it's nice to meet you!"

"I've never met a spectral being before. How intriguing."

It seemed the girls weren't the least bit afraid of ghosts.

Falfa and Shalsha were something resembling amalgams of the souls of vanquished slimes, so in a way, they might be related to ghosts. Both could be called "spirits," anyway.

"I want to see your face, Rosalie. C'mon out."

"I'd like to observe a ghost with my own eyes."

"Sure thing! Okay then, I'll show you my true fo——— Ungh..."

Rosalie's face—technically, Halkara's—had gone very pale.

"Rosalie? Did something happen? From your expression, I'm guessing it isn't good..."

"Big Sis, I possessed her all right, but... How am I supposed to get out?"

That was a terribly basic problem.

"Huh? Can't you do it easily, sort of like closing and opening a lock?"

"See, I've never possessed anybody before. That means I've never left anybody, either."

Was it like an octopus trap? She could get in just fine, but she couldn't get out...

Still, this was no joke.

"Are bad things going to happen if you stay like this?"

Halkara would probably be upset about being possessed for a long time, and it was likely that she had plans for tomorrow.

Immediately, I went to wake up the sleeping Beelzebub.

"Uuuuuhn... What is it? I just got to sleep..."

"We want to get Rosalie out of Halkara's body. How do we do that?"

I assumed Beelzebub would know how to deal with it.

"What? Can't she just come right out?"

Aaaaargh! She doesn't know any more than I do!

"Come here! Come on! Help me think about this!"

"Don't pull on my arm like that! Ow, ow!"

I took Beelzebub over to Rosalie-and-Halkara.

"I can't get out. It's like I fit into a box perfectly, and I can't get loose."

"I wonder if your affinity was too good... I've never heard of anybody being unable to get out."

"Hey, is this going to damage Halkara's health somehow?"

"If a different soul is in the body for a full day, it does put a strain on it. In the worst case, the body will die."

This is incredibly bad!

Immediately, we arranged a family meeting at the table.

"All right. Apparently, the time limit for bringing Halkara back alive and safe is about twenty hours. I want us all to pool our knowledge and resolve this. Seriously, please, everybody help."

Rosalie's color had gotten even worse.

Well, sure. She might end up becoming a murderer.

"I don't want to kill somebody who helped me… If I'm going to end up doing something so shameless, I'll hang myself and die again instead!"

"No, you can't! If you do that, you'll just kill Halkara!"

I talked Rosalie down. *There, there, there. Easy, easy, easy.*

From the look of things, we were going to be up all night racking our brains.

"Um, what about this?" Laika raised her hand first. "If this is similar to an object getting lodged in a box, couldn't we get it out by hitting it?"

"Would a physical blow expel a ghost?"

Beelzebub crossed her arms, cocking her head. True, that was the method they'd used to fix TV sets way back when. But—

"It's better than nothing. Let's try it!"

"Lady Azusa! If you aren't careful about striking her, Halkara will die!"

Oh, right… At times like this, having a status that was too high made things tricky.

And so we decided to have Shalsha administer the blows.

"Hit softly, all right? But hard enough to knock her soul loose."

"Those are difficult terms…"

Even I thought so, and I was the one saying them.

"Here I go, then. I'm sorry, Halkara."

Whap! Whap! Whap!

"Yeow! Owwww!" Rosalie felt the pain, too… Although the body taking damage was Halkara's.

"Well? Do you think you can get out?"

"I kinda don't think so… Ow! Yeowch!"

"Shalsha, stop! We're not using this plan anymore!"

This time, Falfa's hand went up.

"Here, over here! Let's scare her! If she's startled, the Rosalie lady will come out!"

When startled, people always say, "I thought my heart would jump out of my chest." If we surprised her, her spirit might leap out. The problem was how to scare her. And that Rosalie was listening to us talk about it.

"Falfa's got a great idea!"

We decided to put that "great idea" into action.

Using Levitation, I rose unsteadily into the night sky and took Halkara-and-Rosalie along for the ride.

"B-Big Sis, for the love of all that's holy, stop here, okay? This is insanely high…"

"By the way, do you think you can get out now? Or are you still stuck?"

"It's no good… I can't get out of Halkara."

Altitude alone wasn't enough, then.

"No way around it. I'll move on to Stage Two."

"Huh? There's a Stage Two?"

There was no point if Rosalie wasn't startled, so we hadn't told her.

"Mmm-hmm. I'm going to drop you."

"Whaaaaaaaaaaaaaaaat?! P-please, no, anything but that!"

"It's fine. Laika's in dragon form, and she'll catch you."

"S-save me! I-I'm gonna die! The fear will kill me!"

"No worries there. You're already dead, Rosalie, so you won't die of shock… I'm sorry. Halkara's life is riding on this! Oh, if you struggle like that, you'll fall."

"You're going to drop me anywaaaaaaaaaaaaay!"

That was true.

And so I let go.

"Aaaaaaaaaaaaaaaaaaaaaaaaaaaaaaaaaaaaaaaaaaaaah!"

After a nerve-shattering scream, I heard Laika call, "She's safe!"

I descended slowly and checked on the situation.

"Did it work? Did they separate?"

"I thought I was gonna wet my pants, Big Sis..."

Rosalie, her face pale, was sprawled on top of Laika. Her body was still Halkara's.

"So that didn't work, either..."

We tried all sorts of things.

For example, when morning came, we called the village cleric and had him perform a sort of exorcism.

He chanted the blessed words in an indistinct murmur. In Japan, the equivalent would have been having a Buddhist monk come and read a sutra.

"Aaaaaaaargh! I'm dying! This is gonna kill me!"

Since there was a danger that Rosalie would be destroyed before she came out, we stopped him.

It was almost noon, and we still hadn't come up with a fundamental solution.

According to Beelzebub, "Unless we get her out soon, there's a risk that it will start to have a negative effect on Halkara. It all depends on the strength of Halkara's soul, but—"

"We don't have time, but we also haven't slept, so it's getting more and more difficult to think."

Laika was looking droopy, too. How could it be this hard to find a solution?

Falfa and Shalsha were about as drowsy as they could get, so we'd sent them to bed ahead of us.

"I'm tired, too. Still, if we fall asleep now, Halkara's going to die... Wait a minute."

I might have stumbled onto a clue.

"Laika, when Halkara drinks, she always passes out, doesn't she?"

"Yes. At the buffet party, she ended up lying on the floor."

"If we put her to sleep when she has two souls, do you think Rosalie's soul might fall asleep on its own and switch with Halkara's?"

I had no academic basis for saying this. It had just occurred to me.

"True, she has been awake all this time, so having her go to sleep is worth an attempt."

In any case, we had to try everything we could think of; there was no other way. It was the "try or die" mindset.

We gave Halkara's body—currently in use by Rosalie—lots and lots of liquor.

"I've almost never drunk alcohol before…"

"The body's Halkara's, so it's fine. Drink enough for a bath!"

Halkara usually conked out around the fourth glass.

That day, possibly because she'd stayed up all night the night before, or maybe because her body was hosting Rosalie, her face flushed faster than it usually did.

"Huh…? There're five of you, Big Sis…"

She had to be pretty drunk if her vision had gone funny.

Right after she started on her third glass, Rosalie slumped forward onto the table.

After she fell, we watched her carefully, and before long, she slowly raised her head.

"Hmm? I don't remember drinking… And on top of that, it's broad daylight. What's going on?"

"It's Halkara!" "You've returned!" "Oh-ho, so it worked!"

"Huh? Why is everyone looking at me so fondly when I just woke up after getting drunk? …Come to think of it, my body is incredibly heavy. It feels as though something's clinging to me…"

Yes, that's because it is clinging to you.

"If Halkara's mind becomes even clearer, this could work. Possession should be difficult under those conditions."

"But what can we do, specifically?"

We were almost there. We were just one step away from a solution.

What could we do to make Halkara's mind assert itself more strongly?

"Leave that to me! I know how to wake you up to a maddening degree!"

Beelzebub seemed to have hit on something. She immediately pulled on Halkara's hand.

"C'mere a second. Right now!"

"What? But that's the bathroom… Yesterday's bathwater will be cold already."

"That's what makes it so perfect!"

Beelzebub grabbed Halkara and hurled her into the bath.

Kersplooooosh!

Water splashed up, and Halkara's face promptly popped above the surface.

"What are you doing? Oh, honestly! I'm wide awake now!"

"Yes, you are. And that's why you've managed to separate properly."

Rosalie's transparent body was floating behind Halkara.

"Huh…? I'm out?"

As she spoke, Rosalie looked stunned.

"Hooray! The separation maneuver is a success!"

In the end, the method that had done the trick had been to put Rosalie's mind to sleep so Halkara's side would emerge, then do something that sharpened her awareness.

All we'd needed to do was create a situation where Rosalie's consciousness relinquished control due to drunkenness or sleep. When she switched places with Halkara, who'd been behind her, Rosalie wouldn't be able to stay there anymore.

Once we knew the logic behind it, it wasn't that surprising.

"I'd like to investigate a little before we try it again, but it's possible that if we'd simply put Rosalie to bed and had her fall asleep, Halkara would have been the one to wake up, and we could have dealt with it that way. Working all night really wasn't a good idea. It's less efficient."

"Still, if I hadn't materialized in the bathroom when you summoned me, I might not have hit on that last idea. My injuries turned out to be worth it. And since my injuries were hardly injurious, I call this a win-win."

Beelzebub was wearing a hugely triumphant expression. After that achievement, she'd earned the right, so I didn't mind.

With that, the matter had been safely resolved, but—

"I think we're all tired, so let's sleep until five this evening. Everything else can wait."

My opinion was well received, and we all obediently climbed into our own beds to slowly wake up again that evening.

"All right, let me introduce you one more time. This is Rosalie the ghost; she's going to be living here with us."

Everyone had gathered around the table for self introductions.

Despite being incorporeal, Rosalie sat in a chair conscientiously.

Since she was able to make herself visible at will, everybody could see her right now.

"I'm Rosalie. I'm really sorry for all that trouble! Let's be friends, okay?!"

Everyone welcomed Rosalie with applause.

Between this and that, the members of this household were highly adaptable, so before long, Rosalie would probably be able to live here without feeling out of place.

"By the way, are you able to move around inside the house?"

"Yes, I can go anywhere on the property, garden included. Actually, I went outside the garden, too. I'm not sure, but I think I can probably go as far as I want now."

Huh? Weren't location-bound ghosts unable to leave buildings?

"When we moved her, her attachment to the place where she died probably lost its effect. She's got nothing to do with resentment now. She's just a spirit."

True, this place had no connection to Rosalie's grudge.

"Well, that should make things easier for you. Let's see… Go ahead and use an empty room on the second floor of the log cabin area. I say 'use,' but you're a ghost. We'll put things there or take them away to suit your preferences."

"All right! Thank you so much, Big Sis! I won't forget the favor you've done me as long as I live!"

It was a mystery what length of time "as long as I live" actually denoted when the person in question was already dead.

"Um, I don't want to be forward, but… Will there be any changes to the cooking shifts?"

Laika really was earnest. A class-president type.

"The cooking shifts? I doubt Rosalie can cook in the first place."

She could do it if she possessed someone's body, but if the person being possessed got tired, that would defeat the purpose.

"I can, though. Technically."

A cup rose lightly from the tabletop.

"If I can move knives and plates like this, I can cook. I haven't eaten in a really long time, though, so I can't swear it'll taste good."

"I see. It would be helpful if you could cook for us, but… Hmm. Would it really have to be a duty?"

Something about that bothered me a bit.

"Mom, we ask people to take cooking and cleaning shifts because they eat and get the rooms dirty through the course of daily life. Rosalie is a ghost, so she doesn't eat, and she won't make anything dirty. Consequently, it wouldn't be right to give her duties like that."

Shalsha had spoken formally, but that was exactly what had been nagging at me.

Just because Rosalie could do it didn't mean she had to, did it?

"Big Sis, that ain't proper! I'm taking shifts for everything, too!"

Rosalie stood up from her chair. Well, to be accurate, she floated out of it.

"I'm going to be living in this house. Even if I'm a ghost, I'm still living here! In that case, I need to repay the debt I owe by doing that!"

Rosalie's eyes blazed with passion. She looked so lively you'd never have thought she was a departed soul.

"I'm sorry, Rosalie. I had the wrong idea. In that case, we'll have you do what you can do."

True, if someone told you, *You don't have any obligation to us,* you'd feel more guilty than happy.

It was healthier to handle things in ways that didn't leave anyone feeling indebted, and we should be able to get along for longer that way.

"Yes please, Big Sis! The rest of you, too. If you need anything, just say the word! There may be things only I can do *because* I'm a ghost!"

"Uh-huh, thanks in advance!"

"I'd like to hear more views that are unique to spirits." Shalsha seemed likely to start doing full-fledged paranormal research and write something on the subject.

"The same goes for you, Rosalie. If there's anything you don't understand, do ask us."

"Um… Please don't possess me very often, okay?"

After all, to Halkara, it was a matter of life and death… Still, ghosts were scary because you couldn't see them, and now that Rosalie was visible, Halkara had probably come to accept her.

"If I run across any more information on ghosts, I'll look it over and bring it to you. Well, for the time being, I doubt you'll have trouble."

"We're in your debt again, Beelzebub. And you were busy, too; I'm sorry."

"I was the one who resolved this, so you made the right choice in calling me."

I'd better give Beelzebub a present next time. I think she'd be really happy to get a year's supply of Nutri-Spirits.

"All right, that's settled for now. Why don't we have a party to celebrate our new family member?!"

Still, before I got up from the table, Rosalie distracted me.

She was crying. Actually, it was fair to call it "wailing."

"What's the matter? What happened? Did you remember something bad?"

"It's just... My own parents betrayed me, and you saved me even though we aren't blood relatives..."

Her tears of joy fell to the floor.

However, they disappeared the second they made contact. There was no physical moisture in ghost tears; they existed simply as a manifestation of Rosalie's emotion.

You know, this house really may be a space for misfits.

After all, I was an irregularity myself, so if somebody strange came along, I was able to extend a helping hand.

As a matter of fact, I intended to go on making sure I did just that.

"If you live long enough...really nice things happen to you, too, don't they? I'm so happy..."

"I believe you mean, 'If you're dead long enough.'"

Beelzebub landed a flawless verbal jab.

That night, we threw a party to celebrate Rosalie in earnest.

We'd bought quite a lot of things in large quantities for the earlier party for Halkara, so it was easy for us to hold another one.

However, since the guest of honor wasn't able to eat, we kept the food simple.

"There are places that are hard for human hands and eyes to reach, you know? I can use a rag to wipe them down!"

Rosalie was making a point of identifying the ways a ghost could come in handy. Everyone had something they could do. It probably wouldn't be long before she was indispensible to our highland cottage.

After that, Rosalie went over to Halkara and gave a deeply courteous bow.

"I put you through some awful trouble, Sis Halkara! I'm real, real sorry about that!"

"Oh, it wasn't so bad… I was unconscious, and I don't really remember what happened to me anyway. Although I did dream about Shalsha hitting me a lot and getting dropped out of the sky."

Those things actually happened…

"Um, Sis Halkara? Please hit me until you're satisfied."

Rosalie stuck her head forward.

"I-I'm sorry; what is this about?"

"I caused you trouble, so if you don't hit me, the scales just won't balance!"

"Honestly, don't worry about it! Hitting isn't really my thing…"

Halkara was embarrassed. Rosalie really did have the temperament of a gang member.

"Go on, Halkara, hit me!"

"I told you, hitting people holds no interest for me! Frankly, I think I'd prefer being hit."

What was she saying?!

"Er, well, I've only had that thought about eight times in my entire life! It's an aberration!"

That was a strange number of times…

"Also, you're a ghost, so I can't hit you anyway. That means this conversation is over."

Halkara wrapped things up cleverly. Yes, that was about the neatest possible way to shelve the matter.

"Besides, if you want to make amends, I'd rather you did something that benefitted me. Rosalie, you can see places that other people can't because you're a ghost, correct?"

"Yes, if it's something like that, I can do as much as you want."

"In that case, help me when I go to gather medicinal herbs. In the forest, there are many places I don't notice right away, and there may still be some herbs I haven't seen yet."

"Yes'm! I will most definitely help you out!"

Ooooh! Nice job, Halkara! She's got a proper understanding of Rosalie's unique talents!

Then my daughters approached. People seemed to naturally gravitate to Rosalie.

"Say, Miss Ghost? Is there anywhere you want to go? Falfa will take you there!"

Come to think of it, Rosalie had been in that house all this time, so she hadn't seen the outside world in ages.

"Let's see… I've been shut up inside, so I'd like to go someplace with a pretty view. I think I'd like to travel, too."

"Uh-huh! Come take a trip with us, then!"

I didn't know whether you could call her "shy," but for a girl who'd been cooped up like Rosalie, someone as outgoing as Falfa might be perfect.

"I'd like to hear more details from you about how ghosts see the world. I'm very interested. And intrigued."

Yes, that was what would be on Shalsha's mind.

After all, there weren't many opportunities to talk with real ghosts this way.

"Actually, I think I'd like to visit the spirit world."

"That's scary, so be a little more careful, would you?!"

I couldn't have Shalsha dying on me, so I broke into the conversation.

"It's fine to be interested, but make sure you come home, all right?! It's not okay to just stay gone!"

"Yes, journeys are possible precisely because one has a home to return to."

That was all well and good if it was true, but researcher types really did tend to take things to their natural extremes.

"Either way, I don't know anything about other ghosts, so I can't really introduce you. I was always on the lot where my house used to be, by myself."

So Rosalie really had been truly alone.

In that case, I should probably let her meet lots of people.

"Okay! I can't call it a journey, but let's start by tackling something close to home."

$$\diamondsuit$$

Right away, the next day, I took Rosalie to the village of Flatta.

If I'd said I wasn't nervous, though, I would have been lying.

After all, most people had never seen a ghost. They might be frightened. Maybe they would avoid Rosalie and make her feel bad.

Even so, I didn't think it would be good to keep her hidden away. In this case, if we were going to get people to understand her little by little, it would be better for us to move quickly. After all, it wasn't likely that people's attitudes toward ghosts would abruptly soften ten years from now.

Possibly because Rosalie understood that as well, she seemed tense.

"Do you think they'll accept me, Big Sis?"

"Frankly, I don't know. Which means I think we'll just have to try it. After all, if you only go from being cooped up in one place to being cooped up in the house in the highlands, you'll be lonely, won't you?"

"No, compared to the days when I was all by myself, there's a world of difference. I'm grateful to all of you."

Rosalie's reply made me happy. Curses! If she had a physical body, I'd be hugging her right now! How could she be un-huggable?! It's fraud!

As it turned out, Rosalie and I were worried for nothing.

"Oh! So you've added a ghost to your family this time, have you?"

"How 'bout that. If she isn't another beauty!"

The villagers received us quite naturally. They weren't the least bit scared.

"Big Sis, is everybody in the world this friendly? I feel like a moron for spending so much of my time as a ghost in that building by myself..."

"You know, I was fairly sure they'd be a little less welcoming than this, but..."

Rosalie and I looked at each other, nonplussed by how well it was going.

Afterward, when we went to greet the village chief and I told him about it, he laughed. "Ha-ha-ha! Well, of course. After all, none of you folks has ever been normal, you know? No one would be scared of a ghost this late in the game. To us ordinary mortals, you're all birds of a feather."

"Frankly, I'm pretty sure you're right."

Rosalie seemed likely to blend in to the village without any trouble at all.

Very soon, Rosalie began going down to the village or into the woods whenever she found some spare time.

Since she'd been shut inside for so long, everything seemed unusual and novel to her.

Oh, and since we couldn't put Rosalie in charge of a cooking shift right away, we had her help the rest of us during our shifts.

At first, she'd only been able to chop vegetables roughly, but her technique was getting better and better.

Being able to wield a knife easily also gave her some pretty powerful combat specs.

"Yes, those are nice thin slices! At this rate, you'll be able to make an onion salad, too, with a little improvement."

"It's all thanks to your teaching, Big Sis! Damn straight!"

What's this "damn straight" business...? I'm still not used to delinquent culture. And wait, she was alone all that time; I wonder where she learned about delinquent culture to begin with. Is it something you acquire automatically all by yourself?

"After this, I'll tackle the space above the ceiling! I'll use a wet rag and clean it properly!"

"That ability is a tremendous help. Please keep it up!"

Thanks to Rosalie, the sanitation in this house was on track for some major improvements.

When you thought of a witch's house, you tended to picture an eerie place in a gloomy forest, but I preferred mine to be thoroughly clean, open, and airy.

We'd experimented with setting up terrace seating at the café, and it might have been nice to have a lunchtime tea party out there.

Besides, if you could become a bit of a celebrity simply by having a tea party on the terrace, it wasn't a bad thing at all.

While Rosalie was beginning to get used to our house—

Halkara was also doing battle in a new environment: recruiting an opening staff for her factory in Nascúte.

However, it sounded as though it still wasn't going well for her. Yet again, she came home with drooping shoulders.

"Ooooh, I see nothing but trouble ahead…"

"Why? We cleared up the Rosalie incident. It's still no good?"

"I am telling people that the ghost problem has been resolved, of course. It's just that no one had actually seen the ghost in the first place, so I can't seem to get them to trust me."

That was a pretty tricky problem.

If there was a big rock in the middle of the road obstructing traffic, the moment you got it out of the way, everybody knew. However, it was hard to get people to understand that a place generally considered to be haunted was now ghost free.

"In that case, why not just show Rosalie to everybody? If they can see her, she won't be as scary, and they'll understand that she isn't there anymore."

"That's it!!!"

Halkara's voice was incredibly energetic.

"Understood, Big Sis! Time to get back to town in style!"

Rosalie, who'd been floating in midair, also sounded enthusiastic.

I don't think "in style" is quite what we're looking for here...

I was worried, so I decided to go along, just to be on the safe side.

And so, in Nascúte, we held a presentation ceremony for a ghost.

"'Sup, people! I'm Rosalie; I killed myself on that street over there, way back when. Right now, I'm living with my big sis, the Witch of the Highlands! I don't live here anymore, so don't go acting like I do!"

"There you have it! She's the genuine ghost who committed suicide on the factory lot! You can see for yourselves how adorable she is; she's not frightening at all! In fact, since we've confirmed that there are no other wandering spirits, you could even say it's safer than working somewhere else! Come one, come all, come work at the factory!"

Rosalie and Halkara were walking around the town, shouting.

"Hey, what's that, what's up?" "They said she's a ghost." "Now that you mention it, she does seem kinda see-through..."

What they were saying was pretty strange, so people had mistaken them for entertainers of some sort, and a crowd had gathered.

"They took the bait. Rosalie, do you mind if they touch you?"

"I'm untouchable."

"No, that's just fine!"

Halkara seemed to have thought of something.

"Anyone who'd like to touch a ghost, step right up! She's authentically incorporeal!"

At that, an old man brought his little granddaughter to touch her.

"Oh, I went right through her!"

The paranormal experience made the girl giddy with excitement.

"See? Don't you go dying, kiddo. Stay healthy, got it?"

"Okay, ghost lady!"

Possibly due to the little-girl effect, the surrounding crowd was looking on warmly. They seemed to have begun realizing that she was a good ghost.

"She ain't the least bit scary, is she?" "She doesn't seem like an evil spirit at all."

Her approval rating was rising. This was a good trend.

Then Rosalie seemed to hit on an idea.

Spotting an elderly couple, she flew lightly over to them.

"Say, you two. Is there anything you're having trouble cleaning?"

"Yes, we can't get at the higher areas of the windows… Even if we stand on chairs, we can't reach."

"In that case, I'll use a rag and wipe those down for you!"

The old couple's faces brightened.

"That would be a great help! Thank you!"

"Go ahead and tell me your address! I'll get that done right now!"

Other people called to Rosalie: "Could you do our house, too?" "There're cobwebs on the ceiling at my place…"

"All right, okay! I'll get to 'em in order, so just sit tight!"

Rosalie's face was shining. It wasn't clear how she was speaking, but I could hear her energetic voice clearly.

"Halkara, even as a ghost, it's possible to live for people, isn't it?"

"Madam Teacher, she is a spirit, so she's not living."

"Don't nitpick."

"It's obviously more fun to have people appreciate you than it is to be hated. I'll work to manage my company to benefit the town as well."

Halkara was sounding like a decent entrepreneur.

In the end, her factory had made one person happy.

After that, Rosalie began visiting the town once a week and helping out by being a tourist attraction.

Go on, work to become the liveliest ghost in the world!

Since Nascúte had accepted Rosalie, Halkara's labor shortage issues seemed to be nearly resolved as well.

"I've found ten people who'll work for me!"

Halkara made her report a week to the day after we'd taken Rosalie to town.

"In that case, the factory should open soon, right?"

"Yes! The Halkara Pharmaceuticals Nascúte Factory has a prospective start date!"

Halkara Pharmaceuticals… Was that what she'd named the company?

"Now I'll be able to start mass-producing Nutri-Spirits again! I'm going to do it!"

Nutri-Spirits was an energy drink Halkara had created that had been an explosive hit in another province.

It had "spirits" in the name, but it didn't have any alcohol in it.

For a long time, Halkara had been using her knowledge as an apothecary to make all sorts of products.

She'd always had a good head for business, and she'd made a huge success of her Nutri-Spirits.

After that, she'd gotten the mistaken impression that the powerful demon Beelzebub was after her and had shut down her local factory, and it had been closed ever since.

"Now I'll make money hand over fist! Naturally, I'll give the profits back to the town! First, I'll establish Halkara's Sublime Water Well so that townspeople and travelers can drink as much delicious water as they want! Then I'll build Halkara Hall and make regular stage plays a possibility! Fifty years from now, they'll have a copper statue of me, I bet!"

I don't think that copper statue is necessary, but if she's doing things that will benefit the town, I approve.

"By the way, do you have a business license?"

Halkara tended to be sloppy about such things, so it was a good idea to check.

"They say the aristocrat who governs the province of Nanterre is picky about money. He hasn't overcharged you or anything, has he?"

The area where we lived was a nice pastoral place, but it wasn't as if the whole province was like that. I hadn't heard many good rumors about its governor, either.

"Ahem! No worries there! I submitted it properly! I delivered it to a Nanterre bureaucrat! There are no problems whatsoever!"

Halkara puffed out her chest as she spoke. If she was acting like this, then she probably had submitted it.

"The only thing was, when I turned in the papers, they asked me an odd question. 'Don't you have a little more of a present?' or something like that…"

"Doesn't that mean they asked you for a bribe?"

"Ha-ha, I guess they do ask you for that sort of thing in this province, don't they?! I don't really understand all that myself, so for the moment, I sent them plenty of edible wild grasses."

Halkara sounded perfectly unconcerned.

"Wild grasses?"

"Yes. Where I used to live, there are certain times when you give each other wild grasses and fruits and things as a greeting. I treated this as something similar and sent about a week's worth."

"And the other party was satisfied with that? I mean, it would be exasperating to just meekly hand them a bribe, too, but…"

I was getting a bad feeling about this.

"Those grasses are delicious, so he'll probably be delighted to get them. They're bitter, but that's part of what makes them so good."

"Um, Halkara? If anything happens, tell us right away, okay?"

Halkara was steadily running up flags. I highly doubted things were going to keep progressing uneventfully.

"Oh, Madam Teacher! You're so overprotective. I'm a grown adult, and really, there won't be any trouble. Besides, we're quite well respected in the area around Flatta."

Yes, in Flatta *and its vicinity.*

Vitamei, the capital city of Nanterre, was pretty distant. Had the information gotten that far? Even if it had, did they believe that a powerful witch and company really existed?

Still, Halkara wasn't picking up on any danger, so for now, I let the matter lie.

Besides, if my fears were groundless, nothing would need to change.

A few days later, Halkara's factory opened for business.

She didn't have many sales outlets at first, so instead of making anything in bulk, she sold her products in Nascúte and the nearby areas and watched to see how it went.

Her product lineup consisted of Nutri-Spirits and other health drinks.

Lots of them had strange names, such as "So Young! Wellspring of Health" and "Sleepiness Smackdown Solution."

All the products made reliable sales.

Even though none of them were familiar, there must have been something about them that caught the eye.

Halkara really did have an incredible knack for marketing, thanks to her accurate grasp of buyers' feelings. One week after operations began, production had doubled.

According to Halkara, if the factory made smooth progress, she'd be doing well enough to build a second plant. She probably had fairly concrete plans for that as well.

As far as I was concerned, as long as Halkara was having fun working, I had no complaints.

As an aside, although Halkara was going to the factory and issuing directions, she eventually wanted to leave all the processes to her employees and become a full-time president.

She really was more of an administrator than an apothecary.

"You know, if this keeps up, buying an entire town may not be beyond the realm of possibility. We're growing quite nicely."

Every day, when Halkara came home, she cheerfully gave us the rundown.

"Here you go, Falfa and Shalsha. I brought you souvenirs. They're rare books; I had people search the province's bookstores to find them."

"Yaaay! You're the best, Big Sister Halkara!" "Thank you, Halkara."

The two of them were genuinely thrilled about getting books they hadn't been able to find.

"Madam Teacher and Laika, I have some people on the hunt for good liquors to give you right now. You celebrated with me earlier, and I intend to return the favor!"

"You're a pretty big spender, aren't you?"

"If you don't use what you earn, the economy stalls! This is proper economic activity!"

To all appearances, Halkara was in fine form.

However—a week later, it happened.

Laika returned one night in a panic.

"Hmm? Laika, you're back earlier than usual."

Laika usually transformed into a dragon to drop off Halkara and pick her up again, shuttling her back and forth between the highlands and the town.

"Terrible news, Lady Azusa! They say the aristocrat who governs the province has arrested Halkara! Apparently, she's suspected of a crime!"

"I did have a bad feeling about that. I knew it!"

We should probably head for the town right away.

I grabbed Falfa, Shalsha, and Rosalie, and we all left for Nascúte on Laika's back.

I would have felt uneasy about leaving my daughters home alone, and I also thought Shalsha might be quite knowledgeable about this country's history and trends.

Stern soldiers armed with spears had blockaded Halkara's factory. They seemed to have come from another city, possibly the provincial capital.

A young woman was eyeing the factory uneasily from a distance, so I struck up a conversation.

"Excuse me. Do you know anything about that factory?"

"Yes, I…I was an employee there."

We'd found a welcome source of information.

"We're Halkara's family. Can you tell us anything?"

The employee took us to her apartment and explained the situation to us there.

"We were operating as usual. Then, after noon, a group forced their way in, saying they'd come to arrest the president on orders from the provincial governor. They said the crime was selling medicine without a license or something…"

"Big Sister Halkara said she sent in an application. I can't believe she didn't have a license."

It was just as Falfa said. I'd heard about it from Halkara as well.

"There's no mistake. This is a conspiracy to arrest Halkara!" I shouted, unusually for me, and the young employee flinched. "I'm sorry. I've never dealt with anything like this before, either."

"No, I was afraid they'd hear us outside. The governor is probably here to oversee the soldiers."

What? In that case, we could negotiate with him directly.

We went to the town government office where the provincial governor was staying.

Even so, there were guards, and they wouldn't let us inside. But we didn't retreat immediately. If the governor came out, we'd be able to talk to him. We might at least be able to get Halkara released.

After a few minutes of wrangling with the guards—"Just let us talk to him for a minute." "No!"—we found the townspeople gathering behind us.

As a matter of fact, I'd hoped that would happen. Generally, the Witch of the Highlands, Halkara's factory, and Rosalie were all spoken of favorably in this town. In that case, we could get the will of the people on our side.

"It's rather noisy out here."

Finally, a man who seemed to be the provincial governor emerged. He had a striking mustache that flared out into an upside-down V.

"I'm Golder, the governor of the province. I'll have you arrested for attempting to release a criminal by force without going through the courts."

Shalsha took a step forward.

"In this case, there is no need to imprison the suspect on the spot. A review of the documents would be enough. Consequently, we request that you release Halkara."

That's my Shalsha! She knows a lot about litigation, too!

"The decision to imprison her was made on the authority of the provincial governor. We took these steps because we had sent a warning but received no response," Governor Golder announced in an arrogant voice.

"That can't be! Halkara wouldn't have continued to operate her factory after receiving a warning!"

Welling with indignation, Laika shouted. It was as if she was expressing my feelings for me.

"If you have any complaints, come settle the matter in court. We've merely followed the proper procedures! If you claim she's innocent, then bring proof of such!"

From behind us, the residents yelled: "Hey, you! You're forcibly arresting somebody who didn't send you a bribe, aren't you?!" "You know full well the courts are in on this with you!" "He's right, listen to him!"

Wow, talk about premodern… It looked like they hadn't separated their legal, administrative, and judicial powers.

Halkara had probably drawn their attention by not giving them that bribe.

"In any case, the inquiry will be conducted in court. Those are the rules. If you have documents that can prove her innocence, you may submit them. Although, even if you do, I'm sure we'll immediately discover that you forged them. Ha-ha-ha!"

Damn that man! He was roaring with laughter. If this was how it was, even if we ransacked Halkara's room and found documents related to that license, they'd probably be invalid and full of glaring problems. Then they'd say they were counterfeit and drive us away, and Halkara's crime would be an established fact.

"Long story short, we received no application. Well, if you donate several tens of millions of gold, we might discover that the document was simply temporarily lost in the shuffle."

So if we wanted to save Halkara, we had to cough up some money, hmm? He was completely underestimating us.

"Aah, I want to hold that trial right away. The factory was operating illegally, and the province will have to confiscate it!"

"No! Halkara poured her heart and soul into that factory! Confiscating it would be too cruel!"

By this point, Laika was so mad that she seemed about to breathe flames. Still, we couldn't use any more force. We'd put ourselves at a disadvantage.

"Governor, if you intend to pervert justice, I assume you're prepared for the consequences?"

I spoke quietly, without letting my emotions show.

"Oh, you're that swindler, the Witch of the Highlands or something like that. You must have amassed quite a lot of money after spreading those rumors that you're the strongest anywhere. I wager you have gold for when it's needed, correct?"

So he knew I existed, but he didn't believe in me. This was an era with no television or Internet, after all.

"Well? If you are 'the strongest,' do you want to try stealing the prisoner by force?"

"No, we'll prove justice in court. The surest victory is a victory by trial, you see."

I'd meant to give a dauntless smile, but in the end, I couldn't manage it. I just glared at the governor.

Smirking, Governor Golder disappeared into the building.

You just made enemies of a family you can't afford to fight.

Our overpowered abilities could be used for things besides combat.

My eyes went to Rosalie.

"Rosalie, I'd like to borrow your power."

"Huh? Me?"

Rosalie looked blank.

"Yes. With your abilities, I know we'll be able to win this trial."

In no time at all, the day of the trial arrived.

Our entire household went to court as witnesses. We were determined to win with an "innocent" verdict. No, we'd win more than that. We'd done what we needed to do to make it happen.

At last, it was time for the court to open.

The chief justice and four lay judges entered. The chief justice would direct the proceedings, and the results of the trial would be determined by a majority vote among the five of them. Many of these people had ties to the provincial governor. That meant that this wouldn't be anything close to fair.

By the way, we'd used Shalsha's connections to hire a pretty important person as our lawyer.

Governor Golder had also taken a seat. Apparently, he was planning to watch the proceedings.

We were about to teach him what happened to people who got on our bad side.

Suddenly, a lay judge who was presumably connected with Governor Golder stood up.

"Okay, so like, I...I mean, to my mind, she's innocent. After all, this makes zero sense! We can't go admitting things that make no sense! That's just logic! The sun sees all, you know!"

The lay judge wasn't talking like a lay judge, and a stir ran through the court.

Yes, that's right: that was Rosalie in there. I was pretty sure we wouldn't be losing this trial.

After all, we had Rosalie. She'd been able to sneak in and collect all the documents we wanted.

"I'll show you proof that this accusation makes no sense whatsoever! Get this: We found documents that show that the defendant, Halkara, actually did send a form to the governor! In other words, this ain't no crime!"

The elderly lay judge, possessed by Rosalie, brought out the document with a flourish.

The court was instantly plunged into chaos. It was likely that nobody had seen this development coming.

He really should have destroyed it beforehand. Our opponent had played a poor endgame.

"It's obviously a forgery! It can't really exist!" Governor Golder yelled.

After all, if this turned out to be the real thing, it would become an issue of liability on the governor's side. Of course he'd get desperate.

"Well, you see, we've already had thirty legal experts write testimonials stating that it's the real deal. That would be these!"

This time, the Rosalie lay judge whipped out the testimonials.

We'd used Shalsha's connections for those.

Shalsha was acquainted with several liberal arts university professors, and we'd had all of them write testimonials. Since it actually was a completely genuine, un-falsified document, everyone had answered "Yes, that's real" right away.

"Frankly, thanks to these, the truth is as plain as day! Halkara had a license to run her factory and to make medicine. There's no way that's a crime! If you think you can make it one, step up and give it your best shot! —And now I need to make a little trip to the john."

After a pause, we heard a *sploosh* from outside.

It was the sound of Rosalie diving into the pond in the courthouse garden.

Now she should have been separated from the lay judge's body.

—Then she possessed the next one.

If she'd stayed inside one person the whole time, it would have seemed unnatural.

After a little while, the soaking wet and rather mystified lay judge resumed his seat.

Then the second lay judge launched into a monologue.

"Whoops, this lay judge has kept all sorts of records! Every one of them is proof of the governor taking a bribe! Well, if that don't beat all!"

Again, the mood in the court turned strange.

"Those are fabricated! It's some kind of conspiracy!"

Governor Golder screamed. His face had gone pale. He couldn't let something like this go.

"Except that those legal experts have also guaranteed these as documentary evidence. I'm not talking one or two people here. You can't get away with calling something a fake in the face of numbers like these!"

"When did you people steal those?!"

"Steal? You mean you had them? Are you saying you knew the documents existed but claimed they didn't?"

The governor wore an expression that said, *Oops*.

"The villain's shown his true colors. It looks like the jig is up, hmm?"

Just then, somebody made a hasty entrance. He was probably the governor's subordinate or something like that.

"Big news! We've just received a letter denouncing the governor, jointly signed by aristocrats and politicians!"

We'd sent the documents proving that Golder had taken bribes on a tour of his political enemies. Our enemy's enemies had indeed been our friends, and everyone had been delighted to cooperate.

With Laika's speed, we'd been able to collect signatures in a few days.

Since this was all based on clear proof, we could attack as much as we wanted. The lawyer and the prosecuting attorney had nothing to do.

The event had morphed into a Crush the Crooked Governor party.

"All right, defendant Halkara. I bet there's quite a lot you want to say, so let 'er rip!"

Halkara nodded slowly, then stood up. The words *This is totally in the bag* were written all over her face.

As a result, she seemed to have switched into battle mode, too.

"Ahem. I certainly did fill out the documents and turn them in. Then they asked me for a bribe of some sort. I don't really understand these things, you see, so I didn't send a proper one. Then, for some reason, I was suddenly arrested. Groundlessly. Wild herbs won't grow without ground, you know. We can't have that. However, the fact that the lay judges have shown flawless documents is a tremendous help. As far as I'm concerned, I hope the judgment of heaven will smite the wicked, and that's about the size of it. In addition, once I'm given permission to do business again, I intend to keep selling Nutri-Spirits and my other products, and I'd be honored to have your patronage. That's all I have to say."

That last bit was just advertising.

Either way, the matter was settled.

However, the finishing blow hadn't yet been struck. Someone else who seemed like a governor underling rushed in.

"I have an announcement! A crowd has gathered in front of the courthouse…and they're demanding fair trials and the governor's dismissal."

This was because we went to every related office and begged.

This crooked governor had made a lot of people angry. They'd only kept quiet because none of them had the strength to fight him alone.

And so we'd gathered a crowd that was big enough to let them speak.

The bulk of them were from the areas near where we lived, Flatta and Nascúte. Around here, if I made a request, it would go through almost unconditionally. The villagers and townspeople had worked to gather people from other areas to join the demonstration, too.

Our victory was complete.

The prosecuting attorney did say that the trial was in confusion and should be reconvened, but if you looked at it another way, that meant that reconvening was the only move he could think of.

Since the documentary evidence was perfect, the governor couldn't insist that it was all hooey, so he blurted out that he'd forgotten the documents. At that point, Halkara's innocence was confirmed.

Of course, that wasn't the end of it.

Golder declared then and there that he'd resign, but if speaking honestly was enough to get you forgiven, we wouldn't need the police, and he was arrested the moment he left the courthouse.

The incident had been safely resolved. Halkara was innocent, so she was released right away.

"Y-you saved me… That was so scary…"

As soon as she saw my face, Halkara teared up. She'd been toughing it out by herself for a long time. She must have been really anxious.

I patted Halkara's shoulders and hugged her.

"You don't have to worry anymore. The bad guy's gone."

"Thank you so much, Madam Teacher…"

Behind me, our other family members were watching Halkara and looking worried.

"You see, Halkara? It wasn't just me. We all worked together to help you."

This time, everyone had played a part. Shalsha had contacted scholars, while Laika had helped everyone get around by turning into a dragon. Rosalie had possessed the lay judges and exposed the governor's evil deeds, and Falfa had gone to visit with Halkara and encourage her.

This victory truly had been the result of family team play.

"Thank you, everyone, really. I've learned how harsh society can be…"

I'm not sure that's quite what that expression means.

This time, Halkara hugged Laika.

Ordinarily, Laika wasn't fond of physical contact, but apparently, this was a special case, and she accepted the hug meekly.

"Wickedness has been punished. No one will come after you now, Halkara."

"I love all of you! Family really is important, isn't it?"

She hugged Falfa and Shalsha, too, one in each arm.

"Big Sister Halkara, you did a good job!"

"Thank you, Falfa! Those pancakes you brought me were delicious!"

"I'm glad we were able to meet again without incident."

"Thank you for your help, too, Shalsha!"

Yes, very good. Uninterrupted family time. It had been hard, but now that it was all over, you could call it the perfect opportunity to prove our unity.

Then I sensed another presence.

"Sis Halkara… That must've been real rough."

An unknown old guy stood there.

Who's that? He looks like he's of fairly high rank, but... Oh, I guess he's one of the lay judges.

But what was that "Sis Halkara" business? Ah! ...So that's what it was.

"Um...? And who might you be, sir?"

Halkara looked blank.

Rosalie was still possessing the old guy. That was the only possible explanation.

"I'm so glad you're safe! That's just great!"

Still in an old man's body, Rosalie went to hug Halkara.

"Argh! Wait just a minute, please! If a man is going to hug me, I need to prepare myself emotionally! Aaah, you smell...unique. And elderly..."

Because the body still belonged to the lay judge, yes.

"Rosalie, wait, wait! You're not out yet! That's someone else's body!"

Hastily, I tried to stop her, but Rosalie was too worked up to listen.

Actually, she might have been even quicker to tears than Halkara; her eyes were moist. The girl seemed very tenderhearted...

"I'm so glad we saved you... I caused you a lot of trouble just a bit ago, and I was so worried, really worried... I'm so glad!"

"Ouch, ouch! Your whiskers are scratchy! That hurts! What is this, a new type of mental attack?!"

True, having some strange old guy come up and cling to you would be traumatizing no matter what gender you were. Even if I were male, I wouldn't want that.

"Huh? That's weird... I'm starting to feel funny."

"Um, Rosalie, what's the matter?"

"Well... Hugging Sis Halkara like this is making my body go all warm. I'm getting real excited, if I gotta paint the full picture for you. It's almost like it's not my body."

That's because it isn't.

"Is this love? No, we're both women; that couldn't be it... I'd kinda like to hold you for hours, though."

"Because that's a male body! Those are male instincts! Please just get away from me, would you?!"

"Male? Oh, I'm still inside the judge... I'm so sorry, Sis Halkara!"

After that, Rosalie managed to get out by pouring well water over her head.

Halkara kept holding her cheeks for a while.

"Ugh... That scratchiness is a nightmare. Under torture like that, I think I'd confess to things I hadn't even done..."

"Sis Halkara, I'm so sorry. Deck me later!"

Ever picky about vertical relationships, Rosalie was bowing like mad.

"Well, you're a ghost for one thing, so I can't hit you, and even if I could, I wouldn't. You made an incredible contribution to this, too, Rosalie."

If the lay judges were in on the con, all we had to do was force them onto our team instead. Which was why we got some help from Rosalie.

"All right, let's say good-bye to this courthouse already, shall we? We're going home together."

We'd come all the way to Vitamei, the provincial capital, for the trial.

"Yes, let's. The bed in that prison was hard..."

As she recalled the awful environment, Halkara looked dejected.

"Still, you do need to say thank you one more time."

"To whom?"

"In a word, to 'everyone.'"

When we left the courthouse, lots of villagers and townspeople who'd rushed over for today's event were gathered outside.

Some people had even unfurled pieces of cloth with things like Miss Halkara Is Innocent and The Governor Is Corrupt written on them.

"Our family members weren't our only allies. There were many more people who believed in us."

"Oh... Now that's a sight to move one to tears..."

Halkara seemed to regain her energy as she gazed at her supporters. Then the crowd spoke in unison.

""Miss Halkara, you did your time like a true professional!""

"…I actually am innocent, all right? Please don't get the wrong idea!"

$$\diamond$$

In part because the provincial governor had fallen from power, Halkara's incident became a pretty popular topic.

Of course, when I went to the village of Flatta, people flagged me down to offer condolences ("That must have been awful for you"). Apparently, people spoke to Halkara over and over in Nascúte, too. Well, that was the actual site of the factory, so it was probably to be expected.

In addition, people seemed to be sharing the incident all over the province.

I hadn't gone to confirm that, but Shalsha had connections to all sorts of scholars. If she said it was happening, it probably was.

It would be scary if this led someone to set their sights on "the Witch of the Highlands" again, but I hadn't used brute strength to resolve the issue. It wasn't as bad as it could have been.

If I'd retaken Halkara by force, this could have turned into an all-out war… What made this family terrifying was that we probably still could have won.

"Shalsha benefitted as well. There were professors I've been wanting to contact for a while, but I'd kept my distance because I was embarrassed. I sent letters to them, too, and now we have a connection."

"How about that! Shalsha, that's wonderful."

It didn't really show on her face, but as her mother, I could tell she was happy.

"Thanks to that, I got the opportunity to have them read my dissertation."

"Your dissertation?"

Shalsha set a sheaf of about thirty sheets of paper down on the table.

The top sheet had the words *Theory of Slime Culture—Shalsha Aizawa* written on it.

That "Aizawa" was there because my last name used to be Aizawa. However, since I came to this world, almost no one called me anything except "the great Witch of the Highlands" or "Lady Azusa," so I'd almost never been called by it.

"I've explained the culturally historic significance of slimes, point by point."

"That's incredible... Shalsha, you've been doing something like this? Imagine that. You don't just read books, you create them yourself..."

I had no idea whether the content was accurate or not, but it looked like a legitimate dissertation.

"It's grounded in the latest research trends, and I think it turned out well."

"Wow. By the way, about how many people are researching slimes?"

"From the angle of cultural history, there are two in the kingdom, including me."

"That field is beyond specialized!"

It didn't seem like it would bring in much money, and since you couldn't make a business out of it, maybe the people who could engage in it were limited.

"At present, the idea of bringing together the slime researchers in each field and holding a slime academic conference is gaining momentum. If held, it will be a big step in the history of slime research. Shalsha has high hopes for it as well."

"I see... Well, good luck."

People used to research all sorts of things in Japan, and that was true of this world as well.

I might end up attending an academic conference like that one as Shalsha's escort.

"Now then, Shalsha, I'm going to do a little cooking today. Would you come help me?"

It was almost time for lunch, and I should probably get to work.

"Help?"

"Yes, it's been two weeks since Halkara got out of jail, and I think it's about time we had a special meal to acknowledge what she went through."

Even though it had been for only a few days, Halkara had been torn from this house and probably suffered in the process. I wanted to hurry up and recolor the experience with good memories.

"That's a splendid idea. Shalsha would really like to help you with that."

"Good. I think I'll ask you to cut up the vegetables."

After we'd been doing prep work for a while, the guest I'd called arrived.

"I'm here."

Beelzebub was here with a big box on her back.

"What's in the box?"

"I stopped by Nascúte first and bought a crate of Nutri-Spirits."

"You're like a kid with the wallet of an adult! Talk about a heavy user!"

"This'll last me awhile. Although I'll be going back to buy more in three days or so. I'm glad that factory's switched over to mass production."

With such enthusiastic fans on its side, the factory probably wouldn't go under.

"It was commendable of you to call the biggest Nutri-Spirits lover among demonkind. If you'd summoned me when Halkara was arrested, as well, I would've torn that evil governor limb from limb in a jiffy."

"That's why I didn't."

It would have been a much bigger problem if we'd gone overboard and people started thinking, *Demons are scary, and the witch who hangs around with them is scary*. To make matters worse, Beelzebub was a Nutri-Spirits fiend, so I really doubted that she'd forgive anyone who'd falsified charges and stopped the factory.

"Since it's a special occasion, I'll make a demon dish for you. First, I'll steam these potatoes and mash 'em."

The preparations for the dinner party proceeded smoothly.

Laika and Falfa also joined us after we started, and Rosalie took up a knife and chopped vegetables. There were lots of stews and hot-pot dishes this time. We just stewed everything.

"The dish I'm making is demon home-style cooking. It's called 'hot pot from Hell.'"

There was nothing homey about that name, and it sounded spicy.

"It includes some rather hot ingredients, so it'll make your tongue go numb."

"What, so it actually is spicy?!"

"Eating this warms you right up, and it's good for your health. You get the runs the next day, though."

Don't make stuff like that in other people's houses.

As Beelzebub put the ingredients she'd brought along into the pot, its contents grew redder and redder.

If nobody eats this, things are going to get awkward, so I wish she'd made something more orthodox.

Though I had my misgivings, time passed, and then...

"Lady Azusa, it's time to pick her up, so I'll be going now."

It was time for Laika to go get Halkara.

"Yes, please do. The food's ready!"

Now all that was left was for our resident elf to experience the touching sight of all this food.

However...

Although we waited a long time, Halkara didn't come back.

The food gradually cooled. We'd reheat it, so that wasn't a problem.

"Hey, Azusa. You don't suppose she's been arrested again, do you?" Beelzebub asked.

"She can't have been. Not even Halkara would... Well, she is Halkara, so I can't swear it couldn't happen."

After all, "trouble" and "Halkara" did tend to go together.

I hoped she hadn't ended up with a major incident on her hands.

"Actually, your province's governor was fired. What's the new one like? If he was friends with the former governor, he might try to make an example of you."

I had very little interest in politics, and I hadn't even thought about the next governor.

"His predecessor was reckless enough to pin a crime on a friend of the Witch of the Highlands; he didn't know how scary you are. This one might well make the same mistake."

"What do I do?! What if Halkara's been killed or something?!"

"I'd love to say you're overthinking it, but…"

The delightful atmosphere was rapidly deteriorating into gloominess.

"Calm down, Mommy! Laika's gone to get her. If something's wrong, she'll come right back."

Falfa's words soothed me a little.

"You're right… Let's wait for Laika. Right now, that's all we can do."

That said, without the guest of honor, we didn't even feel like making idle small talk.

The overall mood was as heavy as lead.

Finally, it was two full hours past the time Halkara usually returned home.

"Aaaah… Halkara's late, huh."

Falfa had started to yawn. What should we do? She'd gotten sleepy…

"Um, why don't those of us who are here now just go ahead and eat? After all, there's plenty of food."

"Shalsha will wait."

My earnest younger daughter didn't agree.

"I want Halkara to eat her fill of my hot pot from Hell, so I'll wait, too."

If she filled up on that, wasn't it guaranteed to give her the runs…?

"The longer we wait, the more the spiciness soaks into the ingredients, so it's only going to get better. It's the type of dish that's tastier on the second day. There's no problem."

Halkara... Even if you do come home, Hell itself awaits you.

Then it was three hours past her usual return time.

"Zzzz...snkk..."

Falfa fell asleep.

There was no help for it, so I draped a terrycloth blanket over her.

I considered taking her to her room and putting her to bed, but if it made her late to the party and she wasn't able to participate, Falfa would be sad. I decided I'd wake her up when Halkara got home.

"Hmm, I dunno about this... Do you want me to go take a look?" Rosalie asked.

"But ghosts can't travel through this space at high speeds, can they? It wouldn't be good if you missed each other on the way."

"I'll go improve the hot pot from Hell. Actually, maybe I should call it "hot pot of perdition" now; they say that one's even more super-spicy."

On that note, Beelzebub headed for the kitchen. *I give up. Go on, make it as hellish as you want.*

Still, she really was far too late. If she didn't come back after another hour, we should probably at least check to make sure she was safe. I didn't think she'd lose any fights if Laika was there, but I had no proof that horrifying beings didn't exist in the world.

Just as I was thinking that...

I thought I heard the beating of dragon wings.

Hastily, I dashed outside.

It was Halkara, riding on dragon Laika!

"I'm late... I'm sorry..."

Shakily, Halkara got down from Laika's back.

"What on earth happened? You look exhausted."

"You remember that we have a new provincial governor, correct?"

Wait, had he actually retaliated somehow?

"Well, that new governor liked Nutri-Spirits and the rest, and when he took them to the kingdom, apparently His Majesty liked them as well, so… We received a formal order from the Crown."

"From the Crown?!"

"And then the meeting ran long… Since it was a request from the national government, we couldn't really tell them to come back tomorrow, so… We ended up working a lot of overtime."

"If I'd known we'd be delayed this long, I would have returned to the house temporarily, but I didn't know how late it would end up being. I apologize. I misjudged the situation."

Laika, who was in human form again, bowed her head. It hadn't been her fault at all, so I wasn't concerned about that.

"Oh. Well, then. Basically, this was a good problem to have."

I shouldn't have worried.

"Honestly, I'm dead on my feet. I don't need dinner tonight; I'd like to go straight to bed."

"No, we can't have that."

I took Halkara into the party venue.

All the food was laid out neatly.

"Hmm? What's this?"

"You've been through a lot, so we decided to hold an appreciation dinner for you. It's quite a bit later than we'd planned on, but…"

"Madam Teacher! Thank you so much!"

Halkara pulled me into a tight hug. I was getting used to it, but that chest of hers really was impressively resilient. It was one of those things men tended to like. Actually, it could make women pretty happy, too. At my all-girls high school, several of my classmates would just come up and squeeze your boobs.

"Hey, what cup size do you wear?"

"What do you mean by 'cup'?"

I see: There was no unit of measurement for bust size here. Although, even without one, it was immediately obvious that hers were big.

While I was talking with Halkara, Falfa woke up.

"Huh? Halkara, you're home?"

"We're all here! All right, in order to congratulate Halkara on surviving the trouble, and to pray for the further growth of her business, let's celebrate!"

We passed out glasses to everybody.

""Wonderful work, Halkara! Keep it up!""

Halkara's eyes were getting a little teary.

Her face was beautiful and mature, and she seemed a little different from the comic relief character I knew.

"Thanks to all of you, I'll be able to manage as president. Really and truly...thank you so much..."

"Go on, eat up! You are the president, so they'll forgive you if you commute like one tomorrow and get there late!"

"All right! I'll eat absolutely all of it! We just finished a big project, so this feels a bit like a wrap party!"

Just then, a seething, furiously roiling pot arrived.

"I took the spiciness up to level ten," Beelzebub said ominously.

"Um...Beelzebub? What might this dish be?"

"It's hot pot from Hell, demon home-style cooking. Do eat it—I insist. It's my present as a Nutri-Spirits fan."

Beelzebub spooned the deep-red hot pot into a dish.

"But isn't this spicy?"

"Don't you worry. It's not lethal."

That wasn't a word that should come up in connection with food.

Nervously, Halkara took a bite.

"Oh, it's not really all that ho— Aaah! It built up! It hit me something awful!"

"There's still lots and lots left. You said you'd eat all of it, and I was terribly pleased to hear it."

"Wait! I got caught up in the moment! I didn't know this was here!"

"You can't possibly be telling me that you can't eat my cooking, can you?"

Oh. I know where this is going, and I don't like it.

"I'm all full, and I think it's about time I called it a night…," I said.

"I as well," Laika added.

"I'm a ghost, so I can't eat. What a bummer."

"Falfa's sleepy, so I can't eat very much…"

"Shalsha was taught that it's best to avoid eating directly before bed."

"You're all casually attempting to escape, aren't you?! S-save me!"

The next day, Halkara had an upset stomach that kept her from going to the factory.

Still, when things were busy, it was important to rest properly and get your body back in working condition. By the way, because of that spicy food, Halkara had drunk an unusually small amount of liquor, and she didn't have a hangover at all. By and large, it had probably been good for her health.

"Haaah. Maybe I'll make a beverage that helps when you've eaten spicy things…"

Halkara drank a homemade medicinal blend of mushrooms and herbs, and sighed.

It was the morning after the party for Halkara.

As I was making breakfast for the family, Beelzebub returned after having been outside for some reason.

"Where did you go?"

"I meandered around the area a bit. The air in the highlands really is nice and brisk. Especially since I drank yesterday, it'll help me make a fresh start."

A morning walk sounded alarmingly wholesome and un-demonic.

"Back when we were at war with this country, people often said that demons appeared at night, but nocturnal lifestyles aren't good for you. Among the demons, I advocate rising and turning in early."

"I'd really hate to live in a world where you had to be prepared for demons first thing in the morning. Let's keep it peaceful, okay?"

"There are no plans whatsoever for going to war, so don't you worry. Just as your country has no intention of occupying the demon lands, we don't think we could control all the territory on this continent. It's far too inconveniently vast. In terms of serving the administration's citizens, too, what we have now is perfect."

Even from just this conversation, it seemed safe to assume a demon invasion was next to impossible.

"Ah, right. They've settled on a date for conferring the Demon Medal. Do come and accept it."

"Oh! You mean the thing about the peace division, right?"

I'd stopped a conflict between dragon tribes once, and for some reason, the demons had been impressed. As a result, they were granting me this award.

Apparently, it was prestigious, but without any connection to the demon world, I didn't know the details.

"In that case, I'll accept it gladly. Just let me know the date and time."

I wasn't an office worker, and this wouldn't conflict with my job; on that point, I was really blessed in my current lifestyle. When I had been a corporate wage slave, work had actually come in abruptly on the day of a concert once, and I ended up having to eat the cost of my ticket.

The date Beelzebub told me was three weeks away. That was pretty close.

"All right. I'll tell Halkara to take that day off from the factory."

"Yes, I'll have all sorts of food ready and waiting for you."

At the word *food*, I got a bad feeling.

"Um… Don't tell me that every last thing demons eat is hot."

Yesterday, Halkara had choked and said, "My lips are swelling up… I'd like you to put some honey in this, please," as she ate the hot pot. If everything was spicy, we'd be in trouble.

"Relax—not all our food is spicy. If you prefer sweet things, I'll make sure to keep the focus on those."

"Thank you. Cuisine does differ considerably from region to region, after all."

If they went to the trouble of making food for us and we ended up not being able to eat it, we'd feel bad, too.

And so it was officially decided that we'd attend the Demon Medal award ceremony.

I'd never been to the demon lands, so I was rather curious. Long ago, I probably would have been nervous, but from the way Beelzebub looked, we weren't likely to have any problems.

However, Halkara was anxious.

"I have nothing but misgivings about this. Is it all right if I just so happen to get a stomachache that day?"

"You're so scared that you'd fake an illness?"

"They'll probably serve peculiar food, won't they...? She said they wouldn't give us anything spicy, but I wonder if she didn't just mean 'it'll be less spicy than that other thing'..."

The awful experience had made her suspicious.

"Huh? Big Sister Halkara, you're faking sick?"

Apparently, Falfa's ears had caught the word.

"Falfa, that was only a figure of speech. I just think my stomach may start to hurt that day, coincidentally."

Halkara's trying to play this off...

"It's okay!"

Falfa thumped her chest with a hand.

"Falfa can keep secrets! I swear I won't tell the demon-people that you're not really sick! Trust me! I'll tell everybody you're not faking!"

"Don't! If you go out of your way to say it isn't a feigned illness, it will look suspicious!"

"Falfa knows just how you feel, Halkara, so you don't need to worry! The food Beelzebub made hurt, didn't it? You didn't like it very much, and that's why you're not going this time, right?"

"W-well... If you put it that way, you're technically correct..."

"I'll tell Beelzebub for you, but I'll be casual about it!"

Cold sweat began to trickle down Halkara's forehead.

I patted her on the shoulder.

"Halkara, I'd give up if I were you. If things go on this way, Falfa may really tell people you faked sick and stayed home. There's no guarantee that the demons won't hold it against you."

"You think so, too? I really don't like the way this is going. This is one of those cases where she says she'll never ever tell and then goes and tells, isn't it…?"

I think there was a joke routine like that in Japan, too. Maybe it's universal?

"All right. I'll properly attend, with the mindset of someone leaping from the spire of Carrard."

Citing an idiom that apparently was a more vivid version of "taking the plunge," Halkara decided to go along.

Since our entire family was now attending for sure, I'd consider it a good thing.

"We can probably just use the dresses we had tailored for the dragons' wedding, so there's no problem there."

But my family had grown since then.

"I'm sorry, Big Sis." Rosalie floated over to me. "I don't have a dress."

"Oh yes, I see. In that case, we'll go to the village or the town again and buy— Hang on."

How did one buy clothes for a ghost? Could she even put them on?

"Come to think of it, you always wear those town-girl clothes. Can you change them?"

"I've been in this outfit ever since I became a ghost. I'm not even sure how I'd change into something else."

Yikes! That's not a problem I expected to run into!

I didn't know what to do, so I asked Laika and Shalsha.

The two of them seemed as though they'd be knowledgeable about these things.

"Do you think there are shops that sell clothes for ghosts?"

"I really haven't the foggiest idea."

"I've never even seen something like that in a story."

So it was a no-go, hmm? Still, it would be mean to make her the only one in the group to attend in her everyday clothes…

I tried asking at the clothing shops in town as well.

"Clothes for ghosts…? Ghosts can't pay, so it wouldn't be much of a business."

That's what they told me. *I see. That's reasonable.*

Even if they made clothes for ghosts, it wouldn't last as a business, so it was likely that nobody did it.

Next, I used Shalsha's connections to visit an academic authority who seemed informed about ghosts.

This was what the white-whiskered scholar told me:

"It's said that ghosts are souls that have remained in this world, and that they look very nearly as they did in life. For that reason, although they may appear to be wearing clothes, what you are seeing is part of the soul. Not being able to change a soul is perfectly natural. As a consequence, there is no decent way to make them change their clothes."

When I heard that, it made sense to me.

What looked like clothes were actually Rosalie's memories from when she was alive.

If Rosalie had worn an elegant gown, and those memories grew stronger, maybe she would be able to "wear" it, but it was almost impossible. At any rate, gowns were formal clothes, so it would be hard for them to win out over memories of everyday outfits.

Even if it was only for a few days, I'd searched quite seriously, and it was Rosalie herself who stopped me.

"Big Sis, that's enough. If it can't be done, it can't."

"Rosalie, you're thinking you'll just have to grin and bear it, aren't you? You haven't done anything wrong, though. It's not right for an innocent person to suffer."

When I had been a cog in the corporate machine, I'd put up with far too much, and that was the same as giving up on thinking. If people just put up with everything, civilization would be eternally stuck in the Stone Age.

"Besides, if you could, you'd rather get all dressed up like everybody else, wouldn't you, Rosalie?"

When I asked her, Rosalie hesitated for a little, but she eventually nodded.

"If I had the chance to, then yeah, I would, but—"

"I knew it! Then let's keep looking for a way! We shouldn't give up so quickly!"

"But…how are we going to find one? It's not like there are any spells that weird."

"That's it!" I shouted.

"We'll just use a spell!"

"I doubt there is one, though…"

"As a great man once said, if the lesser cuckoo won't sing, I'll make it sing."

"What's a lesser cuckoo? Is it like a cockatrice? Those can petrify stuff…"

"Oops…just forget about that. That was my past life talking."

Right away, I decided to create a spell that would change ghosts' clothes. If it didn't exist, I could just make it myself. I'd put my overpowered witch abilities to work.

However, when I started checking into it, I immediately realized that this was going to be brutally hard.

A spell that affected ghosts was pretty unique to begin with. Using one to change clothes was even more exceptional. There were absolutely no similar spells.

Besides, since the spell would directly interfere with the ghost, if things went horribly wrong, I ran a risk of actually hurting Rosalie.

Even with my overpowered status, this might prove to be a tall order…

Time passed in the blink of an eye, and the day of our departure was approaching.

At this point, we'd be leaving the house in two days.

However, I'd made progress with the spell, too.

I'd found a clue, and I supposed if I did it this particular way, it would probably work.

Now all I had to do was implement the idea.

I handed Rosalie a dress.

It was white, and the design was as simple as possible.

"Here you go, Rosalie."

"Um, Big Sis? What should I do with this? You can show it to me all you want, but I can't put it on…"

"Examine that dress thoroughly and get its image fixed solidly in your mind. Next, imagine yourself wearing it. Make sure the image is vivid, as if you're really wearing it and walking around a party venue. Think of it as visualization training."

Rosalie didn't seem to have caught my meaning yet.

"Big Sis, have you finally resorted to spiritualism? 'Those who believe shall be saved' and such?"

A ghost thought I was being occult. That didn't sit right with me somehow.

"I came to the conclusion that we can probably use a spell to reinforce what you imagine. Then, if we can switch your current outfit for an image of you wearing a gown for about two days, your appearance should change, too."

My serious expression seemed to have motivated Rosalie.

"All right, Big Sis. I'll make sure your enthusiasm pays off."

"That's the spirit. After all, those who believe really will be saved!"

And so Rosalie began to study the dress and conduct some rigorous visualization training around the clock. I had her gaze at the dress from every angle, then stroll through the house, pretending she was at a party.

"There's a buffet party going on here, a buffet," Rosalie muttered. She made Laika jump, but in a way, it was normal for ghosts to startle people. That was probably all right.

Then, finally, it was time to cast the spell.

I drew a rather strangely shaped magic circle in the garden.

It was in the shape of an oval. Ordinarily, the closer these were to true circles, the better.

Apparently, this type was better at affecting ghosts. It had taken some serious research to figure that out.

Rosalie stood just outside the edge of that magic circle.

We'd set the dress on the ground right in front of her. That way, she could keep visualizing it until the very last minute.

"Here I go."

"All right. Go ahead, Big Sis."

I cast an original spell.

"Illuminate the darkness that yawns between this world and the next. Let the outstretched hand catch the other side…"

The chant ended without incident.

Now, the question was whether it would work or not. It was the first time I'd used this spell, so I really had no idea.

"Work properly, spell! Change, Rosalie!"

It had no direct bearing on the spell, but I shut my eyes and shouted loudly!

Then, timidly, I opened my eyes, and—

There was Rosalie, wearing the dress.

Actually, it was more magnificent than the dress I'd given her, with splendid lace trimmings.

"Oh, ohh… Big Sis… It worked! Now I'll be set even if there's a ball!"

Rosalie was almost in tears.

They were contagious: I was crying, too.

"I'm so glad! Now you'll be able to wear a fine dress to the demon lands! Except for the way you talk, you're a regular princess!"

"Thank you very much!"

We hugged each other tightly. Rosalie was a ghost, so my arms slipped right through her, but I wasn't going to care about little things like that. This was how we hugged, period. It was an air hug.

"Big Sis, can we fine-tune this a little?"

"Hmm? Did you want to add something to the dress?"

"I was thinking I'd like to put words on the back, like 'Rosalie In the House'…"

Oh, I'm definitely vetoing that suggestion.

FALFA AND SHALSHA

Spirit sisters born from a conglomeration of slime souls. Falfa, the older sister, is a carefree girl who's honest about her own feelings. Shalsha, the younger sister, is considerate and attentive to others. They both love their mother, Azusa.

HALKARA

A young elf woman and Azusa's second apprentice. Everyone in the family (particularly Azusa) admires her periodic bouts of maturity and her enviably perfect looks... That doesn't change her role as the family member with a knack for screwing up.

BEELZEBUB

A high-ranking demon known as the Lord of the Flies. She frequently shuttles between the demon realm and the house in the highlands, both to get the Nutri-Spirits Halkara makes and to dote on Falfa and Shalsha as if they were her nieces. She's Azusa's reliable "big sister" surrogate.

Finally, the day of our departure for the demon lands arrived. That said, we were all in the house in our everyday clothes.

Beelzebub was scheduled to come pick us up.

From what we heard, it was going to be quite a long trip, so we'd change into our dresses over there. Rosalie was the only one who was already wearing hers, thanks to the spell.

"It's about time, isn't it? I mean, we didn't settle on an exact time, but…"

I'd been reading a book until Beelzebub arrived, but I couldn't seem to relax.

"I expect she'll be here soon. I'll go make sure everything's locked up for the third time."

Laika was terribly diligent, so she'd checked again and again to be sure the windows and the back door were locked.

It was seriously unlikely that any thief would enter this house, but I would feel so icky if one did, so it was better to lock everything up tight. Oh, and I'd also put up a Crime Prevention Barrier spell like the one I'd cast on the village earlier.

"Don't let the demons hate me… Don't let them hate me…"

I wished Halkara would try a little harder to enjoy this.

Falfa and Shalsha were simply looking forward to going out, and they couldn't settle down, so they were wandering around restlessly.

Abruptly, the sunlight that had been streaming in dimmed.

I thought a really thick cloud might have gotten in the way, but even after we waited a little while, it stayed dark outside.

Wondering whether we were in for some rain, I went outdoors and looked up, then realized that that wasn't the reason.

"What is that?!"

Something unbelievably huge, something beyond enormous, was blocking the sun.

A space battleship? No, we couldn't possibly be going into space. Besides, it also looked as if it might be a living creature.

The rest of the family came out to see what was going on and started at the sight.

"Laika, do you know what that is?"

"A demon...perhaps? A few things about it rather resemble the dragon race, but..."

Just then, someone descended from the sky.

As the figure got closer, I recognized Beelzebub.

"My apologies for keeping you waiting. I've come to pick you up. Now, I'd like you to get up on top of this thing. It would be a job and a half to land it here, so Laika, you turn into a dragon and carry everyone up to the top. After that, it'll fly us to the demon lands."

"Beelzebub, what *is* that up there?"

The enormous *something* completely covered the sky.

"It's a leviathan."

"Huh? Wasn't the leviathan a sea monster?"

"There is a theory that leviathans are a type of dragon, Mom," Shalsha told me, ever knowledgeable.

"I don't know whether they're kin to dragons or not, but leviathans are ultra-large flying demons. Sometimes they submerge themselves in the ocean when they're on vacation; that may be why people think they're sea monsters."

"I just can't get over the scale."

What in the world did this creature eat to keep itself alive?

The nonflying members of our group rode on Laika's back, and Rosalie and I ascended to the leviathan using our own flying abilities (although whether you could call it "flying ability" in Rosalie's case was up for debate).

As you'd expect from such a huge creature, its back was broad and flat.

Several buildings had been constructed on top of it.

I'd heard stories about people mistaking whales for islands, and this might have been similar.

"In a way, are leviathans sort of deluxe passenger ships...?"

"That guess isn't far off the mark. All right, let me show you to the rooms for honored guests. You are welcome to go out on deck, but take care you don't go past the safety railing and fall. It may look flat, but when the leviathan moves, it can get steep on you all of a sudden."

"Mom, this is terribly exciting."

Her expression hadn't changed much, but Shalsha's pen was racing across the notebook she'd brought along for note-taking. She was probably planning to jot down her own record of the leviathan.

First, Beelzebub took us to the rooms—or rather, the building—for honored guests.

The creepy face-like things in the decor were apparently just part of demon architecture.

Aside from those, there was an expensive-looking carpet on the floor and a grand table. There were several beds, too, all lined up.

"Leviathans can't travel that fast, so you'll be spending the night here."

"So you'll be entertaining us while we're in transit, too."

"We also took your culinary preferences into account and built the menus around poultry and vegetables. Nothing's spicy, either, so relax."

Oh, good. It sounded as though Beelzebub was trying to match our pace.

"The second floor is a dining space and the third is an observation area. Anyone who'd like to enjoy the view from the sky can head up there later. Now I'll show you the buildings next door."

Our family filed after her.

The next building housed a casino, or something like it. There were all sorts of apparent card games and board games set out.

"Is this a gaming house?"

"That's right. You've got the gist of it. However, we aren't opening it this time, both because you are the only guests and because it's awfully dangerous."

Halkara looked disappointed.

"What do you mean by 'awfully dangerous'?"

"If you get carried away and lose big here, they'll strip you of all your possessions. Demons always play for keeps. They won't lose on purpose just for honored guests. Many have lost their entire fortunes at this casino, then lost the rights to themselves and ended up as debt slaves."

Beelzebub shot a glance at Halkara.

"If somebody like Halkara lost everything she had after I'd called her here, it would be quite awkward."

Halkara must not have heard that, because all she had to say was, "Ohh, if there was a casino, I'd double my money."

If she'd ended up losing her factory instead, we would have had trouble, so I was glad it was closed…

Then we moved on to the next building. It really wasn't much of a stretch to say there was a town on the leviathan's back.

I knew right away what this place was. After all, there were two changing rooms, one for men and one for women.

"This is the great bath. Soak at your leisure until we land."

"Nice. We'll be taking advantage of this place later."

"Since we're here, want to take a peek? Nobody's bathing right now."

We went through the changing room and into the bath. We did take off our shoes, but nothing else.

And then, for some reason, somebody was already there.

"Huh? I didn't think anybody would come in at this hour…"

She looked like a young woman, but the appendages growing out of her head told us she probably wasn't an ordinary human.

But who in the world would be riding on this thing?

"Hmph. You are on duty, girl. Would you quit slacking off and do your job?!"

"I'm sorry, boss."

The young woman bowed her head.

The girl, whose name was Vania, got out of the bath with a splash.

"It's a pleasure to meet you. I'm Vania the leviathan. I'm currently in human form, but my older sister, Fatla, and I take turns flying and doing maintenance work. It's currently Fatla's turn to fly."

The explanation was fine, but it was being delivered by someone who was stark naked, which made it hard to relax.

Still, she was lovely and lean. She looked almost like a doll.

"Vania, don't talk in the nude! You look like a barbarian!"

"I'm terribly sorry, boss!"

Vania plopped herself back in the bathtub.

"Oh, just so you know, this hot spring water is 'demonic,' so do be careful with it."

"Demonic? I've never heard of that hot spring type before."

The only ones I knew were "alkaline" and "slightly acidic."

"Let's see. Long story short, it makes your skin smooth."

"Oh yes, that's pretty common at hot springs."

"However, if you fall asleep in the bath and stay for hours, you'll melt."

Yikes!

"Of course, that's only if you stay in for hours on end. I really doubt there's anyone who'd stay in the bath for seven or eight hours at a stretch, so you don't really need to worry about it."

Laika put a hand on Halkara's shoulder.

"Halkara, don't go in by yourself, please. I'll go with you."

"Ah! I know where this is going; you're failing to trust me again, aren't you?!"

I could see her falling asleep in the bath and being discovered as a gloppy soup the next morning. I'd have to take steps to ensure that that didn't happen...

"Halkara, it sounds as though the demon lands are a place where careless mistakes can have irreparable consequences. Be a hundred times more careful than usual, please!" I implored her.

"A hundred times? All right... I'll be careful!"

If I put it that strongly, surely even Halkara would make a serious effort.

"Vania is also in charge of the cooking. Since you're here, go over that for them as well."

"Of course. For today's meals, I'm planning to focus on poultry."

That was more ordinary than I'd expected. They really were thinking of us.

"We got in some good cockatrice eggs, so I'd like to use those."

"Huh...? Is cockatrice edible?"

You could technically call it poultry, but was it all right to eat? It hadn't caught on in the human world at all.

"Laika? Have you tried cockatrice?"

"No, I have no experience with it, either."

"Cockatrice eggs are exquisite. Their shells are purple, but the contents look very similar to chicken eggs. Absolutely do try them. And so you know, the ability to petrify has been selectively bred out of these cockatrices!"

How one would remove the petrification ability from a cockatrice was a mystery, but it had probably been similar to the process of breeding wild boars into pigs.

"We also have a roc egg!"

That was even more preposterous!

"Aren't those gigantic?"

"Yes. They're too large, so the cooks divvy up the egg among themselves before they bring it onboard. We have a contract with a roc who lays good eggs, so expect something wonderful."

"You've got a contract with the roc itself…"

I'm going through all kinds of culture shock here…

"The vegetables are also first-class specimens cultivated by alraunes, so they're extraordinarily sweet, and I believe you'll be able to enjoy the innate flavors of the ingredients. Do look forward to dinner!"

Vania wore a cheerful smile. I didn't know her actual age, but that smile made her seem very young.

If I remembered correctly, alraunes were a type of plant spirit race who could move around freely. Apparently, the demon lands were home to a wide variety of people.

"All right, Vania, make sure you prepare a written apology later for taking that bath during work hours."

Beelzebub spoke casually, wearing a smile that was very similar to Vania's.

"What?! No, but…I gave a proper explanation, too, so please let me off."

"Nope. When you do something careless, it becomes my responsibility as your supervisor. Write an apology for skipping work. Got that?!"

Watching the crestfallen Vania out of the corners of our eyes, we left the bath. If we stayed there, she wouldn't be able to get out.

"That's about it for the tour, I think. Now, since we've got the chance, do you want to go to the observation area? The view is more interesting before it gets dark."

We went to the third floor of the building in which we'd be spending the night.

The observation area was not a deck but an ordinary room.

In exchange, devices that looked like binoculars pointed in every direction.

"Wow! What a view!"

The kinds of sights I'd seen long ago from the window of an airplane spread out before me.

The mountains and towns looked incredibly tiny. From this angle, you could see that most of the country was green. The area covered by towns was really small. People were living very close to nature.

"Aaaaaaaaaaah! What is this?! My head...! It's spinning!" Halkara wailed.

"Oooooh! Shalsha, come and look! Look!"

"This scenery should be recorded. I'd like to write about it later."

"So we're this far up? Guess even this isn't high enough to reach heaven, huh...?" Rosalie mused.

While everyone else cheered and shouted with joy, Laika was calm.

"Laika, you sometimes climb to altitudes like this on your own, don't you?"

"When you fly below the clouds, lightning strikes can be dangerous, so I stay as high as I can during those times. It decreases my risk of colliding with my kin or with the roc birds you mentioned earlier."

As I listened to that, I thought, *Dragon common sense really is uncommon.*

"That's about all I had to go over with you. If you need anything, just tell Vania. I'll be working in the staff administration building, and I'll come back when it's time for dinner."

"Sure, thanks. I didn't think your hospitality would begin while we were still on the way to the demon lands."

Even as a witch, I wasn't often treated to service this flawless.

Well, no matter how hard the villagers or townspeople tried, they couldn't put a leviathan in the air, so that was to be expected.

"It just goes to show how great your achievement was. They don't mobilize a leviathan for simply lending a helping hand. You stopped a long-running dragon conflict. That's enough to let you leave your mark on history. You could afford to act more important than you do, you know."

The way she was praising me left and right was kind of awkward.

"I'll do my best not to embarrass myself during the ceremony."

We relaxed in our room, and before long, it was time for dinner.

As an aside, it sounded as though Beelzebub would be eating with us. So this was going to be a dinner party with a high government official, I guess?

Vania brought the food in on a table with casters.

"Here is today's dinner. We'll begin with a salad made with twenty different types of vegetables!"

It was a collection of brightly colored vegetables with a rainbow of hues, plated in an aesthetically pleasing design.

It was possible that more emphasis had been placed on visual enjoyment than on taste.

"Oooh, it's gorgeous right from the beginning."

"Yes. Cuisine for the guests of demons is expected to create an initial impact with its appearance. We pay particular attention to the plating of anything that can be arranged into a pattern," Vania explained.

"This one is in the shape of a magic circle that operates on others' minds, you know," Beelzebub added.

That wasn't exactly encouraging...

"Eating it won't hurt you one bit. It isn't spicy, either, so relax and enjoy."

Sure enough, it wasn't spicy, but there seemed to be all sorts of herbs in it, making for a flavor I wasn't used to.

"Mph... Falfa isn't sure she likes this very much..."

"Sister, if you're picky about what you eat, you won't grow. Urgh... It's bitter..."

Apparently, the salad was a bit too much for children.

"Oh, you poor things... Vania, fix something the two little ones can eat instead!" Beelzebub ordered. She really spoiled my daughters.

"Y-yes, ma'am!"

A dish of fried chicken drizzled with honey sauce promptly presented itself.

If she was able to respond to an order like that one, her skills as a cook were clearly formidable.

"Uh-huh, this is yummy. ♪"

"Delicious… I could eat this all day."

I'd really rather they ate a few more vegetables, but this was banquet fare, so maybe I could let it slide.

"Next is a potage of mashed beans. A variety of spices has been added to this dish in order to camouflage the herbal overtones."

The flavor was pretty complex, and spicy to boot. It had a sort of traditional flair to it.

"It burns a little. Falfa doesn't think she can handle this."

"Sister, there are too many things you've neglected to try. Ooh, it hurts a bit…"

The kids weren't used to this flavor, either.

You probably had to be an adult before you could consider flavors like this one delicious.

"Vania, bring out something else for those two!"

"But there isn't time to prepare a soup at this point…"

"There must be fruit back there. Make up a fruit plate!"

"Y-yes, ma'am!"

Vania ran off again, then brought out four types of sliced fruit topped with a sweet sauce.

"Yes, Falfa really enjoys the sweet stuff!"

"It has a pleasant acidity to it. I don't think this is something you'd tire of eating."

Vania sighed with relief. "Phew… That's good to hear…"

This might generate quite a bit of stress for the kitchen staff. I'm really sorry…

"The next dish is scrambled and seasoned cockatrice eggs. To eat them, you wrap them in lettuce leaves. Oh… If the young ladies aren't fond of lettuce, they're welcome to go ahead and eat them plain."

"Mommy, can we do that?"

"No. Eat at least that much properly. If you don't, it's rude to the person who's serving it to you."

As you'd expect, I did make them eat the lettuce.

"Next are omelets made with roc egg! The velvety flavor is superb, so do savor it!"

This time, Vania brought out the omelets with an attitude of complete confidence.

I'll dig right in, then. I'm very particular about my omelets.

"This may be the most delicious egg dish I've eaten in my entire life!"

The flavor's incredibly rich! Not only that, but the more you eat, the more robust the flavor gets!

"I had no idea that omelets of this caliber existed... I must apply myself more..."

Laika was astonished, too. After all, omelets were her best dish.

"There's no help for that, Laika," Beelzebub replied. "The quality of the ingredients is of a different caliber. It costs a thousand times more to make a roc omelet than it does for a normal omelet."

"A thousand times?!"

That figure shocked Laika, too.

"Yes, so of course they're delicious. Frankly, if Vania made something nasty-tasting with ingredients like these, she'd have to write another apology."

"Ngh... There's no slacking off under you, Lady Beelzebub."

"Somebody who was taking a bath is in no position to talk!"

Beelzebub was a strict supervisor, it seemed.

"That was really quite delicious. You weren't kidding about keeping the dishes egg-based."

And now we'd finish up with dessert, hmm? Not bad at all.

"No, there's plenty more to come. Next up is baked mutton wrapped in pastry. Vania, bring it out!"

"Yes, I'll get it ready right away!"

Wow, there's more...

After that, they brought out about five more courses, not counting dessert, and I got pretty full.

Falfa and Shalsha were holding their round bellies.

"I ate way too much...," Halkara said, drinking herbal medicine that was good for digestion.

"Thank you, Vania. That was an impressive spread."

"No, no. It's my job to be as hospitable as possible. I'm delighted you enjoyed it."

I thought this demon had done very well. She looked refreshed, as if satisfied that she'd given her best effort.

"True, with regard to entertaining guests, I give you a solid passing grade. Well done, Vania."

"Thank you very much, Lady Beelzebub!"

Vania smiled and bowed in response to the compliment. It was things like this that made me realize that Beelzebub's status was nothing to sneeze at. As far as demons went, she outranked the leviathans.

"That just about does it for most of your duties."

"Hmm? Was there something left to do? Oh, did you mean the washing up?"

"No, that written apology."

"You haven't forgotten about that, ma'am?! I just assumed that you'd forgiven me because the food was good..."

"Are you daft? Those are two completely different matters. Turn in something wonderful enough to melt *my* heart. Your words must ooze contrition. If you don't, I'll lower your evaluation, so keep that in mind. And that wasn't a joke. I'm serious!"

"Understood, ma'am..."

With eyes like a dead fish, Vania retreated.

"You're hard on your subordinates, aren't you?"

"It's her fault for slacking off in the bath when she was on duty. If you'd been upset about that, it could have turned into a political issue. This is only natural!"

When it was warranted, Beelzebub took people to task properly.

That day, we slept in magnificent beds.

Since we were all in one big guest room instead of separate rooms, I had the rather unusual experience of sleeping in the same space as everyone else.

However, a slight problem peculiar to travel reared its head.

When we'd all been in bed for about twenty minutes, Shalsha stirred restlessly.

"Mom… I can't sleep in strange beds."

I see. Yes, Shalsha does have a sensitive side.

"What about counting sheep?"

"I already tried it, but my mind went to the iconographic significance of shepherds, and then I really couldn't sleep."

I understood her thoughts had taken her somewhere complicated, but not much else.

All right, this seems like a good time to be motherly.

"In that case, Shalsha, do you want to come sleep with me? You can get into this bed."

Shalsha nodded.

As she slept, she clung to me tightly.

Hugging things seemed to be very soothing for people. Which meant it helped them sleep well.

But then Falfa—who'd seemed to be sleeping without trouble—woke up.

"I'm thirsty, so my eyes just opened…"

Inns have better ventilation than ordinary homes, so you often ended up getting thirsty.

"Huh? Shalsha's gone. Where'd she go?"

"Shalsha's sleeping here with me."

"No fair! Falfa wants to sleep with you, too, Mommy!"

Well, yes, that was probably inevitable.

"Sure. That's fine. Quietly, though—if your voice is too loud, you'll wake up other people."

"Okay!" Falfa said loudly.

In response to the noise, Laika groaned a little and almost woke up, but she went back to sleep. *Good, good.*

Falfa also hugged me. As a mother, it made me happy, but did it make it easy to sleep? Not really...

"Big Sis, do you want me to sing something for you?"

Rosalie drifted over. Since she was a ghost, she didn't need to sleep.

"No, that's okay. I think it would actually wake me up."

As we were talking, Halkara bolted upright in bed.

"Once you get thirsty, you wake up right away, don't you...?"

Apparently, it really wasn't possible to sleep soundly in an unfamiliar bed.

"I brought some incense that lets you relax and sleep peacefully. Shall I use that? Yaaaaaawn..."

"Oh yes, good! Use it, use it!"

When it came to plants, Halkara knew her stuff. She was bound to have some pretty good incense.

Halkara got the incense ready and then commented, "Since I'm up, I'm going to go take an evening bath," and left in a daze, carrying her towel.

All right, this time I'm going to sleep for sure!

The soft fragrance of the incense was unraveling my tension. Yes, this was going to work pretty well. *I'll sleep straight through till morning. Just a little more, and I'll be able to sleep!*

"Uuuhn. Inns do make one thirsty, don't they...?"

This time Laika had woken up.

Since everyone was waking at different times, I couldn't concentrate on sleeping at all!

Even so, I tried again. I really almost made it last time. *I can sleep; I can sleep!*

Then Halkara came in.

"My, but evening baths are pleasant, aren't they? That Vania girl soaked with me. The water was quite nice. I'm all warmed up, so I'll just slip under the covers and go right to sleep!"

They say going to bed just after a bath makes it easy to sleep, in summer or winter. In summer, the heat of evaporation or something cools your body down and makes you feel good, while in winter, it warms you up.

Still, that was true only for the person who actually took the bath.

"Oh, for the love of… Halkara, when you came in, the noise woke me up again."

"I'm sorry! I thought everyone would be asleep by now, and I got careless."

Even so, I had finally grown tired, and at last, I did fall asleep.

After that, all I had to do was sleep soundly, but—

"Wake up, Mommy! It's morning!"

This time, Falfa was awake early and woke me up.

"It is, is it…? If possible, it would have been nice to sleep a little longer…"

On my other side, Shalsha had also begun to stir, so I gave up.

"But the sun's really, really pretty outside!"

Falfa opened the window.

True, you could see the sunrise plainly. The view from far up in the sky wasn't half bad, and my mood naturally lifted.

At some point, Laika had also woken up. "This is nice. It's put me in a sentimental mood as well."

"Hey, why don't we take advantage of this and go to the deck?"

We looked down from the observation area. The leviathan was flying over a wasteland. The kingdom's territory was behind us, and we'd probably be entering the demon lands soon.

It wasn't dreary at all. You could actually have called it majestic.

"Wow. This really does feel like a sightseeing trip. I like it," I said.

"Here I am, a tiny speck in the midst of this vast land. It brings home just how wide the world is."

Shalsha was saying something literary, as she tended to do.

"Falfa's never seen a view like this before! It's really neat!"

The older girl was getting a little hyper as she frisked around.

"I've never flown over a wasteland like this one before, either, so it is a mysterious feeling. It makes one realize just how far it is to the demon lands," Laika said.

"You wouldn't think that a place that's so empty would go on for so long. Even if there are no towns, there are usually forests, or hills, or something."

I'd risen a little earlier than I'd planned on, but this sort of experience might not be a bad thing.

"Big Sis, should we wake up Sis Halkara?" Rosalie asked.

"Hmm... It might be better to let her sleep, but it wouldn't be nice to leave her out of this. Would you go wake her up?"

Halkara seemed sleepy at first, but right away, she began watching the scenery intently.

"Well, Halkara? What do you think?"

"I'm hungry."

Her answer made me laugh.

She was right: Eating was just as important as letting your thoughts travel far away.

After that, it was time for breakfast, so we headed for the dining hall.

However, no preparations had been made. That was odd; had we gotten the time wrong?

After a little while, Beelzebub came along.

"Say, this is when breakfast was supposed to be, isn't it?"

Beelzebub looked around, then squared her shoulders and marched off somewhere.

A few minutes later, Vania came in looking as if she was about to cry— No, she already was.

"I'm sorry! I'm so sorry! I'll get everything ready starting right now, so please wait in your room for just ten minutes!"

Apparently, she'd overslept.

"You do understand what will happen to you if you cause me any more embarrassment, don't you?"

"H-have mercy..."

It was scary when demons got truly angry. Putting somebody to death didn't seem out of the question.

I really hoped this wouldn't result in any pain or bloodshed for her...

"I may have to cut your salary for half a year."

That was fairly rational. It was still a severe punishment, though.

"Please, no, anything but that... I bought some nice furniture this year, and my budget really can't take any—"

"If you have time to haggle with me, finish those preparations! Get to work, and look sharp about it!"

"Y-yes'm... I'm terribly sorry..."

Even if it had been Vania's mistake, I felt a little sorry for her.

"There are a lot of us; can we help? We could probably carry dishes and things, at least."

"Absolutely not," Beelzebub answered immediately. "You are guests who have been formally invited by the demons. If word got out that I'd made those guests do meal prep, it wouldn't just embarrass me, it would shame all demonkind. You must not help, no matter what."

I see, so it's a matter of face.

"By the way, I can shave off Vania's horns and give 'em to you if you'd like."

"No, thank you, but please don't! She looks like she's sorry already!"

"All right. Well, wait just a little longer, if you would. I'll go help with the breakfast prep, too."

Beelzebub headed for the kitchen. It was awful to see two demons so abnormally close to blowing a fuse, but after we'd been told in no uncertain terms not to help, there was nothing else for it. Maybe I'd go back to bed for a bit.

"I did have a bad feeling about that."

Halkara seemed to have remembered something.

"What do you mean?"

"When I went to take that evening bath, Vania was there, you know? I asked her, 'Are you going to be all right in the morning if you bathe at this hour? Won't you need to get everything ready?' and she was very adamant. 'I never sleep in! Have no fear!' That was when I thought there might be trouble."

So apparently, there were demons who were prone to blunders like Halkara.

As far as I was concerned, I'd gotten to sleep a little longer, so I was grateful.

Breakfast was roast chicken wrapped in leaves. A dish wrapped in lettuce had appeared yesterday; did demons like eating things that way?

"This is really good, isn't it? Let's make it at home, Laika. The meat has been marinated in a secret sauce, but except for that, I think we could re-create it without any problems."

"You're right. Let's try it."

My daughters were commenting on how yummy it was, so apparently it was a hit with them, too. We'd learned something good here.

Only Halkara said, "This is delicious, but don't you think the meat is a touch too spicy?"

"That's because I made that meat. We didn't have enough time for Vania to do everything herself, so I cooked, too."

"The parts you were in charge of clearly have a different flavor, Beelzebub..."

It wasn't that the demons liked spicy things. It was just Beelzebub.

After we finished eating, we borrowed card games from the casino and played together as a family. As long as we didn't bet money, we'd be safe. There were lots of different games, so we didn't get bored.

Then, finally, we neared the land of demons, according to Beelzebub.

"You should go take a look from the observation area again. It's pretty interesting."

She was right. It was a remarkable sight.

There was a wall where the demons' territory began. An abnormally thick, high, long wall.

Just how much time had it taken them to build that thing?

"Long ago, I hear the demons were truly afraid that humans might destroy them. As a countermeasure, they devoted themselves to building a sturdy town wall. Frankly, it was a waste of time. The humans never invaded this far, so the wall just sits there."

It was like an amped-up Great Wall of China.

Behind that wall, I could see demon villages here and there. I didn't know how much longer it would be until we reached our destination, but the goal had to be getting closer.

About an hour after that, the "ship" slowly started to descend.

"We're about to land. The leviathan can't touch down in the urban area, so after this, you'll be transferred to a horse-drawn carriage."

So it operated on the same principle as an airport.

At the "airport" on the outskirts of the city, we were loaded into a carriage, and then we finally set off for the castle that acted as the demons' royal capital—an enormous fortress city called Vanzeld.

There were all sorts of demons inside the fortress.

Most of them were horned people like Beelzebub, but others looked like animals walking around on two legs, some like beast-men, and some had only one eye.

"You see, the demon race is really an aggregate of all sorts of races. You can't hear the word *demon* and accurately visualize what one looks like. Also, since the sorts that are too close to animals and slime-like things can't live in the city, in the end, they're treated like wild animals."

"I see. Well, yes, slimes don't go to shops and ask for bread... Although I couldn't say whether they eat bread in the first place."

The city wasn't built all that differently from a human city, and the streets were paved with stone and neatly maintained.

"Now we're entering Vanzeld Castle. Well, strictly speaking, we're in the castle already."

"That's true in fortified cities, isn't it? So the castle town is treated as if it's inside the castle?"

In Japan, there are barely any walled cities, so the common assumption tends to be that castles are located in the middle of town or up on top of hills.

"First we'll have you meet the demon king. The ceremony's tomorrow, so after that, I'll show you around town."

Quite casually, Beelzebub dropped two very loaded words.

Did she just say "demon king"?

"Huh? The demon king?"

When Beelzebub said the word, I responded with a question before I could stop myself.

The idea that we might meet a scary-sounding person like that had completely slipped my mind.

"Well, the medal is presented by the head of state. Obviously the demon king's going to be involved. It's fine; our ruler is a kindhearted soul."

"Th-the demon king… What will I do…?" Ever since she heard the words *demon king*, Halkara had been sweating for reasons that clearly had nothing to do with the heat. "If I slip up, I'll be killed… They'll tear off my skin, then burn me alive…"

"They'll do no such thing! If you insult the demon king, you'll be burned alive!"

So she'll get incinerated after all?!

However, I couldn't deny that Halkara might blunder and incur the king's wrath.

"Halkara, behave yourself, all right? It might be best if you steered clear of anything alcoholic. You might end up barfing on the demon king or something."

In the past, when Beelzebub had been taking care of her, Halkara had come very close to vomiting down her back.

"All right… I want to demonstrate my good breeding… I'll end every sentence with a subjunctive clause, as it were, um, should be."

"That's creepy, so don't."

When Laika had heard "demon king," she'd also straightened up slightly. Apparently, everyone was anxious. Meeting a king was enough to make you nervous on its own, and this was a demon king. It would have been stranger if we'd managed to stay calm.

"You've all begun to look a bit grave, The demon king is a friendly sort, so you can just act as you usually do."

Even if she said that, there were insular types who were friendly to their own people but cold to outsiders, so we couldn't get careless.

"No, the demon king truly is a mild-mannered individual. Demonkind has a few rough types, but as long as our leader is around, there won't be a problem."

So Beelzebub told us, but we were in unfamiliar territory, and we were still a little on edge.

In the midst of that atmosphere, we left the carriage and entered the sturdy stone castle.

However, the building's interior was pretty complicated.

We went outside, then entered again from somewhere else, went underground, then climbed stairway after stairway… *What is this?*

"Why is it such a labyrinth in here?"

"If we do this and enemies invade, we can make them lose their way and wipe them out before they find it again. It's a remnant of the past."

That part did seem a bit demon-like.

"No one ever assumed that a big army would reach this castle. The idea is that if we make them lost, we'll be able to defeat them for sure."

After that, she made us walk for about two kilometers. We had no problems with regards to stamina, but it was significantly taxing.

Then, just about the time our nerves had started to relax…

"All right, the demon king is just past this point."

My back went rigid again.

"So it's time, is it? Proper manners, proper manners..."

If I talked too much, I might slip up, so I'd stay silent as much as possible. I should be able to fool them that way.

"Um, excuse me... I, Halkara, have developed a stomachache."

Timidly, Halkara raised her hand.

"So you finally tried faking sick." Beelzebub saw straight through it. "No need to worry. The demon king will forgive anyone, even you. All right, come on!"

Beelzebub pulled Halkara along after her.

It did look as if Halkara was consciously trying to be careful, so there probably wouldn't be any problems.

Finally, we entered the demon king's hall. Even the doors that formed the room's entrance were about four meters tall. The four demons who were in charge of them worked together to push them open.

"Welcome to the demons' stronghold, Vanzeld Castle."

As we entered, a voice suddenly addressed us from the side.

It was an individual with pretty sheeplike horns on either side of her head. She looked to be about the right age for middle school. Although, yes, that was only her apparent age.

"Oh, hello. We're terribly honored to have been invited."

"And I'm glad to be able to meet you. You're Miss Azusa the witch, aren't you?"

"That's right."

"Wow! The real thing! Please let me shake your hand!"

She squeezed my hand tightly. Maybe the way her tail flicked around was an indication she was in high spirits. It forked into three branches, and it moved in an odd way.

Since I was standing still, the rest of our procession had stopped, too.

"Madam Teacher, if you stay here talking for too long, won't we keep the demon king waiting? I really don't want to end up being impaled more times for each minute we're delayed."

Halkara was completely focused on staying in the demon king's good graces.

"Oh, you must be Miss Halkara the elf! I love your Nutri-Spirits; they're delicious! Please shake my hand!"

This time the girl shook hands with Halkara. She seemed to have a frank personality.

"Ow-ow-ow-ow... Your grip is too strong!"

"Oh, I'm sorry. I didn't control my strength properly. Here, have a Recovery spell."

Immediately, the girl applied the light of a Recovery spell to Halkara. Clever girl.

"Thank you very much. Um... I'm sorry, but do you think you could let us move along? We have to go greet the demon king. I'll be in big trouble if he's like, 'Off with that elf's head,' or something..."

"What? That wouldn't happen. It would be mean."

"Oh, but your values are different from elf values, you know. You may say he's kind, but I take that with a grain of salt. Given the circumstances, I plan to act ladylike and harmless, even if I have to pretend to be a totally different person. In less savory terms, I'll trick the demon king."

"You're going to lie?"

"Not with any ill intent, of course. It's only that such etiquette is an important part of human relationships. You can't just let everything hang out right from the start."

"Listen, Halkara... She's probably someone close to the demon king. You really shouldn't talk about falsifying and tricking, etcetera."

Halkara was careless about these things, and she tended to snatch defeat from the jaws of victory.

"Oops, you're so right. I'm sorry, but do be extra careful not to mention this to the demon king, please. In return, I'll give you three crates of Nutri-Spirits."

Halkara stole a glance at the throne, which was up ahead.

However—and I only registered it then myself—the throne was empty.

Hmm. Hrrrrmmm… What could it mean?

"Um… Beelzebub, the demon king's not here."

"She's right in front of you."

…I thought that might be it.

Pinching up the edges of each side of her skirt, the sheep-horned girl curtsied lightly.

"I am the demon king, Provato Pecora Ariés. I don't really like greeting people from high places, so I came down here."

Well, sure, of course. Of course this girl was the demon king. When I looked around again, except for Beelzebub, almost all the demons were kneeling.

"I…blew…it…"

Halkara had turned white.

She knelt immediately. Actually, what she did was closer to prostrating herself with her forehead on the ground!

"Your Majesty, I'm terribly sorry! What I said about tricking and falsifying—those were just figures of speech! Really and truly, honest! Please believe me!"

She had said some pretty rude things, after all. This wasn't good.

"Huh? Big Sister Halkara, you'd said you were just going to fake sick. Does your tummy hurt for real? Is it making you curl up?"

"They say that sickness begins in the mind. It's possible that she was so intent on faking illness that her stomach actually began to hurt."

Falfa and Shalsha, you're just adding insult to injury right now.

"In the end, I did come here, so please don't say that."

"My, my! You actually considered doing something like that?"

The demon king was still smiling brightly, but that was its own kind of scary.

"No, I—I was merely worried that I might commit some rudeness… King Prot Pakona Elias…"

"Listen, you, the demon king's name is Provato Pecora Ariés," Beelzebub said with disgust.

Halkara froze up. She looked a bit like a frog.

"Lady Azusa, she's diligently accumulating discourtesies. Is this going to be all right?"

Laika, who was watching from behind me, seemed to be getting seriously worried.

I couldn't deny the fact that she might pull off a combination technique.

The demon king crouched down and patted Halkara's shoulders lightly.

"Do get up, please. You aren't my vassal, so there's no need for you to bow like that."

Oh, good. By all appearances, she'd be forgiven.

"While I'm alive, no harm will ever come to any of you."

"Y-yes, Your Majesty! I understand!"

This time, Halkara raised her head energetically, like a soldier.

Whudd.

Her skull slammed squarely into the demon king's chin.

It was a complete surprise attack, which was probably why the demon king fell right over backward.

"Ow-ow-ow-ow... I'm sorry, I wasn't looking up, and I... Hmm? Your Majesty? Why are you lying down? Huh...? Y-you're joking, aren't you...?"

Nobody responded to Halkara.

Silence...

The air had frozen completely solid.

She'd gotten in a flawless attack on the demon king.

"Your Majesty, please pull yourself together! Oh! She's—she's unconscious!"

She probably had a concussion. After all, no matter how strong you were, if your brain got shaken enough, you'd pass out.

Laika began trembling violently even before Halkara.

"Halkara, really, you're unbelievable... You've really and truly done it this time..."

The elf didn't respond.

She'd passed out on her feet. Apparently, her mind was refusing to think.

The demons had noticed the abnormality, and they began shouting.

"The demon king has collapsed!" "Carry her to the infirmary immediately!" "How can this be?!"

Rosalie offered her own perspective as a ghost. "She looks like her soul might pop out. Man, that's not good. If she accidentally leaves, she won't be able to get back."

"Laika… Hey, this is really bad, isn't it? What's going to happen to Halkara?"

For a little while, Laika stayed silent. Then, for some reason, she shook her head.

"Wh-what's that supposed to mean? That's so ominous."

Shalsha tugged at my clothes.

"I haven't gone over the demon legal code carefully, but even by human law, those who harm royalty are generally executed. We can't talk our way out of this."

"No, but that was just, you know, an accident. She didn't do it on purpose. They'll be merciful, won't they?"

"It might not just be Halkara. They may execute Shalsha and the rest of us. That's how serious that was."

"Waaaaaaah! Falfa doesn't wanna diiiiie!"

Falfa started to cry.

Was this the Azusa household's greatest crisis ever…?

Of course, I'll ask Beelzebub! She'll tell us how to get out of this!

Even my lifeline looked ashen.

"If I'd known this was going to happen, I would have let her malinger. Legally, Halkara is definitely going to be killed. This isn't something petty like angering a provincial governor. No one has ever been spared before."

"E-even so, please do something…"

Beelzebub whispered in my ear.

"For now, stay quiet. If you don't resist, all of you except for Halkara are still technically guests, and you'll be taken to your room. You'll be placed under a tight guard, but still. They can't immediately put guests of honor in prison under suspicion of being accomplices, so you'll be placed under house arrest."

"All right, I understand."

"Then, about saving Halkara. There is one way."

"What is it?"

The existence of a possibility at all was a glimmer of light.

"The only one with the authority to stop or overturn the law is the demon king. Right now, Her Majesty is unconscious. If she stays that way, in accordance with the law, Halkara will be found guilty, impaled, and set on fire. At worst, it's also possible that the elf village where she's from will be destroyed."

"You don't need to give me the specifics. Still, I know roughly what we need to do now."

In short, the demon king had to tell them to stop.

"You're saying we need to wake up Her Majesty, right?"

Slowly, Beelzebub nodded.

"With humans, shaking them a little might be enough to wake them, but long-lived demons can stay unconscious for several days. That'll be too late. Even if you end up using force, you have to wake her up."

"Okay, I got it."

"However, I can't openly let you leave your room. It would make them suspect you were accomplices. Do something, but do it from your room."

"A-all right…"

We had no other options.

"About how much time do you think we have?"

"Well, they caught her in the act, so…not much. Understand that it would be within the bounds of reason for Halkara to be a corpse tomorrow morning. We need the demon king to wake up, but there's really no telling when she'll do that."

At that point, some powerfully built male demons came up. They were holding something that looked like *sasumata*, spear forks with U-shaped heads used to pin down fugitives.

"She's the culprit. Take her away!"

The men marched Halkara off, and other demons came up to us.

"For the time being, we'll show you to your room. As a precaution, refrain from going outside."

"Yes, thank you for your help."

...Although I don't plan to just sit in that room and wait.

You can be sure I'm going to get us out of this mess.

Our group—minus Halkara—was taken to the room for honored guests.

It was one room, big enough for all of us to sleep in together, like the room on the leviathan; apparently, staying in one big room as a group was part of demon culture.

"I apologize for the inconvenience, but please avoid going out until tomorrow. Your room has an attached lavatory and bath, and meals will be brought to you at the appropriate times."

On the surface, the demon spoke to us politely, but the underlying message was, *Don't leave this room.*

However, house arrest was a good thing. They wouldn't be watching us all the time, so there were many different things we could try.

Right. All sorts of things.

"Okay. The situation's taken a very nasty turn, but it's obvious what we have to do," I said after I had everyone sit down. "The demon king herself is an understanding person, and I can't imagine she'd die from a single attack like that one. For that reason, I'd like to make a restorative medicine and use it to wake her up. That will take less time than creating a Recovery spell now."

"Lady Azusa, assuming we'll think about how to take the restorative to her later on, how do you intend to make medicine? This is a locked room. There are bound to be guards just outside and in the corridor, too."

I pointed past Laika's face, into the distance.

Laika turned around, then registered what I was trying to say.

"You mean we'll leave through the window and search for herbs to use as ingredients for the medicine—correct?"

"That's right."

I stood up and went to look out the window, specifically down below. We seemed to be on the fourth floor.

"There are no guards here. As long as we can fly, we can escape. We'll go gather things that might make good ingredients for the medicine. If you bring me all the plants you can get your hands on, I'll pick out the ones I can use."

"But Big Sis, where are we gonna find them? Most of the land around here is paved with stone, and there isn't even any grass growing there."

"Rosalie, you go look for some."

"Huh?"

"First, scout the area outside. This is the demons' stronghold. That means there's a good chance of finding vegetable gardens and medicinal herb plots near the castle. They'd need those during a siege. Even if there's nothing like that, there must be ornamental gardens, and I suspect all sorts of plants will be growing there."

Even among castles in Japan, quite a lot of them had arboretums planted next to them these days. Some had probably been created after the Meiji era, but I imagined it wasn't uncommon for feudal lords to use their vast lands to grow a variety of plants.

"Understood! For Sis Halkara's sake, I'll head out!"

Rosalie slipped through the wall and went outside.

For now, I'll pray that there is a plant area. In the meantime…

I opened the door and, as expected, a demon was standing guard there.

"Excuse me, I'd like to take some powdered medicine. Could you bring me a cup and spoon?"

"There is a cup in your room already. However, I imagine you wouldn't want to use the same one for medicine; shall I bring you another, together with a spoon and some water?"

The guard's expression was cold, but he did take my request.

I'd be using these implements to make the medicine.

Then, before the spoon arrived, Rosalie came back. That hadn't taken as long as I'd expected.

"Big Sis, you were right. There's an area in the castle with all sorts of plants!"

"Great! In that case, I'll head over!"

"Lady Azusa, I'll take care of it." Laika had kept her cool, and she stopped me. "If the person who brings your spoon registers your absence, it will complicate matters."

"That's true... But can you fly in that form, Laika?"

"I can transform into this one as well."

Laika's body shifted into a small dragon, about the same size as a person.

"This may not be the time, but that's...that's so cute!"

What is this?! That form would be so popular as a pet!

"Large-bodied dragons can already live transformed into small humans, so it's possible to change into a small dragon as well. Since there isn't much need to do so, I'm not all that used to it, but..."

Actually, I'd like her to stay this way forever, but it would be rude to say that, wouldn't it?

"In that form, you'll be able to sneak out and gather medicinal herbs quietly. Please do, Laika!"

While Laika was gone, I collected the spoon, the cup, and a pitcher of water from the guard demon.

If I was short on anything, I'd use the free tea and other things in the room and make do.

Falfa and Shalsha had nothing to do, so they'd squeezed their eyes shut and started praying.

Little children are praying to you, so please do something about this.

After a short while, Laika came in through the window. Her mini-dragon arms were filled with plants.

"Will this be enough, do you think? In terms of sheer variety, I believe there is plenty!"

"Well done, Laika!"

The plants differed considerably from the ones I was used to seeing in my area. The climate was far too dissimilar as well, so there was probably no way around that.

Even so, several of them seemed to be related species, so I should be able to do this.

"This is similar to thistle, isn't it? And this is a member of the aster family? Okay, this should work."

I ground several of the plants into a paste and used fire to dry some of them.

"Um, Lady Azusa… Will this have any medicinal effect?"

Laika was my apprentice, so she'd noticed something odd about my choice of plants.

"None. It's just very irritating and extremely bitter."

"What?"

"Creatures recognize bitter substances as poison. After all, if poison were delicious, they'd eat nothing but that and die. There are plenty of exceptions, but as a rule, foods that seem delicious or sweet are safe and necessary for survival, and things that taste bitter are not for eating."

Humans had become extravagant, and in an era where it was possible to eat lots of sweet things, this way of experiencing flavor had changed, too. Now some people called the bitterness of beer and fish liver delicious.

Still, that was mildly abnormal given the laws governing living creatures. Children liked sweet cake, and that was how it really should be.

If you followed that basic principle to its conclusion…

"If something bitter is put into your mouth, you reject it and instinctively try to spit it out. That will wake her up…or it should."

Please let this work…

It didn't take me all that long to make the medicine itself.

The cup was filled with a gloppy green substance. You could tell it was probably bitter just by looking at it.

"If we put this in her mouth, I think the extreme bitterness will wake her up."

This sort of penalty game turned up on TV a lot. They'd make people drink tea that was too bitter and things like that.

Since people would get suspicious if she made too much joyful noise, Falfa was using gestures to express the words *"Woo-hoo! It's done!"* without actually saying anything aloud.

"All right, now the question is, how are we going to get this to where the demon king is sleeping?"

"Do you know where she is?" Shalsha asked.

"Frankly, no clue. She did collapse, so I'm not even sure she'll be in her bedroom. She might be in a place specialized for medical treatment."

"Big Sis, I can go through walls! We'll know where she is then!"

Rosalie held her hands in front of her chest, showing how fired up she was.

True, she was probably the right one for the job, but…

"Beelzebub saw you, and it's very possible that the other demons will be able to see you as well. You don't have covert ops skills, either. Won't they find you?" She'd gone outside earlier, so leaving had been easy. If she was searching the castle's interior, though, the danger of the guards finding out would be much higher. "I'm sorry, but Halkara's life is riding on this, so I'd rather do something safer. Besides, if it failed, I'd feel bad about shoving the responsibility onto you."

"All right… You're right… I'm nothing but a delinquent ghost anyway…"

I'd accepted Rosalie's feelings by themselves and turned down the offer. That said, we still didn't have a way to break out of the situation.

Just then, the window rattled open.

Oh, we hadn't shut the window! Had they found out that we'd gone outside? But if they were going to cross-examine us, they'd come in through the door not the window, wouldn't they?

"I'm so glad it was open…"

The one climbing in was Beelzebub's subordinate Vania.

"What are you doing here?!"

"Lady Beelzebub told me to bring this to you. It's a map of facilities related to Vanzeld Castle. The full image is a military secret; there's no documentation, and it's doubtful whether anyone has a good grasp of it, but…"

Vania looked relieved after what was probably a nerve-racking maneuver.

What she'd brought out was most definitely a floor plan.

"Her Majesty is in a first-aid office in that detached two-story building. If you wake her up, things should work out somehow—or so Lady Beelzebub says."

"Thank you! This is terribly important information you've given us!"

Just then, the guard outside the room opened the door.

At almost the same moment, Laika shoved Vania through the door to the bathroom.

"I heard a commotion."

"Oh, I'm sorry. There are small children here, you know, and they were playing…"

"This castle's so opulent it's *amazing*. So picturesque and intriguing!" Shalsha said, trying to force herself to act like a frolicking child. The way she spoke wasn't childlike, and it seemed pretty contrived.

Falfa pulled Shalsha along, running around the room noisily.

"Yaaaay! It's so big! You run, too, Shalsha!"

"Well, this isn't a cheaply constructed building where the sound will reach the floor below, so you may do as you like."

The guard must have been convinced, and he shut the door. *That was close…*

Vania emerged from the room, holding her head. "I banged my forehead."

This girl seemed to find a surprising amount of trouble; she was a lot like Halkara.

"I'm grateful for the map. The problem is how to get here."

There was no way they'd let just anybody into a place where the demon king lay unconscious.

"I have a Transformation spell, but if there are demons who can see through spells, it would be dangerous... I don't think I could fool a high-ranking demon."

"Lady Beelzebub sent me with a plan for coping with that as well."

"Really?! That's incredibly helpful!"

I guess I owe Beelzebub yet another favor. If she ever runs for some sort of political office, I'll have to make a speech supporting her.

Vania took out a headband with two horns stuck to it.

Plus a false tail.

"Put these on and pretend you're a dem— Um, Witch of the Highlands, your face is scary..."

"There's no way these silly little comedy props will fool them! Be serious!"

Come on, this situation is life or death for Halkara.

"No, I am serious. Both the horns and the tail are from wild animals, so you can't tell they're fake just by looking. If you add a hood to hide the headband, it will work out somehow."

"What about the tail?"

"I've brought demon clothes with a hole in the seat."

Hmm... I had issues with this idea, but maybe it was our only option. Besides, if I changed clothes, it would be harder to spot me.

"Put on this outfit, and we'll tell people you're a physician and go to the demon king. I'll guide you. I-I'd really rather not, but Lady Beelzebub ordered me to, so..."

Vania looked depressed, probably imagining something negative.

"If they find out about this, you'll be killed, too, won't you?"

"How did this turn into something so serious? It's a complete mystery..."

It's Halkara's fault. I'm sorry.

"I plan to get as close to the demon king as possible. Do you think we can do it?"

"Yes. The demon king's collapse is an emergency situation, so there's a good possibility that the retainers don't know the detail of which doctor has been sent for. If we say you're a physician, we may be able to get close… Or so I'd like to believe, at any rate."

We had no idea whether this would work, but we'd give it our best shot.

"All right. Vania, lead the way."

"Yes, understood. We'll go out the window, then make for the demon king on the pretext that you are a doctor."

Then I had to leave instructions for the group that was staying behind.

"Laika, if the enemy charges in here, take my daughters and flee outside. I don't intend to lose, so I'll meet you somewhere for sure."

"Yes, and for my part, I'll protect these two, no matter what happens," Laika answered with a dignified expression.

"Rosalie, you go with Laika. Either that or make use of the fact that you're a ghost and run somewhere where the demons won't find you."

"I'll hide in the walls. I don't think the demons will be able to see me in there."

That makes sense. Unless they had X-ray vision, they wouldn't know.

"In that case, I'll pray for good luck for all of you. Pray for luck for me, too!"

I disguised myself, then escaped through the window with Vania.

"All right, now we'll make for the demon king. Please don't forget that you're supposed to be a doctor."

"It's all right. I've got a doctor kit, too."

In addition to the outfit of a medical professional, they'd gotten me a wooden box meant for carrying medicines. I'd transferred the restorative into one of the glass bottles and put a lid on it. Beelzebub was pretty thorough.

As we got closer to the building where the demon king was, we hit checkpoint after checkpoint, but as soon as my companion announced, "I'm Vania, a subordinate of Lady Beelzebub. In accordance with Lady Beelzebub's orders, I've brought a physician," and showed them something like a staff ID, they let us through.

Vania and Beelzebub were genuine demon staff members, so they suspected us less than I'd thought they might.

Besides, if a doctor really had been called and they didn't let her through, there was a good possibility that it would be deemed an unforgivable offense. They had to let us go.

If we kept forcing our way ahead like this, we'd win.

Finally, we reached the building that held the demon king. We got through the checkpoint at the entrance, then went up to the second floor.

A whole gathering of apparent demon executives was up there. Beelzebub was among them.

"Hmm? What are you people?"

A stern male demon executive spoke to us.

"I'm Vania, a subordinate of Lady Beelzebub. I've brought a physician…"

This wasn't a petty underling we were dealing with, so Vania was trembling a little.

"A physician? I hadn't heard that Beelzebub had called one. Something's not right here."

Oops. This wasn't good.

Beelzebub was looking down. Apparently, she hadn't run the story by these people.

"This is in order to save Her Majesty. Could you let us pass?"

Vania spoke up, trying to get through the situation somehow. She was surprisingly gutsy.

"We have a list of the names of the physicians who examine the demon king. What's your name?"

Argh… How should I know?!

"That doctor's horns look pretty fishy to me. Are those false? Let me see."

The jig was up.

Well, I wasn't planning on much jigging anyway, and I wasn't about to back down, either!

"I guess there's no help for it!"

I took off my hood and tossed aside my horned headband.

"I am Azusa, the Witch of the Highlands! I've come with a medicine that will wake the demon king! I'll revive her right now, so clear the way!"

I was here to save people. I had nothing to be ashamed of.

"I didn't know it was possible to be this shady! Comrades, apprehend these two!"

I couldn't just obediently let myself be caught, either.

Immediately, I closed in on a male demon—who had big horns, like the king of the bull demons—and I decked him.

Whudd!

For a moment, the demon doubled over as if I'd broken him. Ordinarily, that would have taken him down, but…

"Why you… What is this human?"

He hadn't even passed out. All the demon executives were big shots.

Well, there was no point in standing around being impressed.

I launched a roundhouse kick next! Then a karate chop, followed by another roundhouse kick!

The attacks struck home in rapid succession, and the demon switched to fighting defensively.

Now's my chance. I got in close and hit him with my fist!

The man had finally lost consciousness. He slumped to the floor, bleeding from his nose.

I took a little breather. My medicine box was in the way, so I set it on the floor and checked out the situation.

There were about ten enemies. Even though she was a leviathan, Vania had been caught with relative ease. Beelzebub was playing innocent—"I know nothing about this, nothing at all!"—and holding the attention of two people who were questioning her.

Even so, there were about five enemies left between the demon king's room and me.

Perfect. I'm doing this.

"Let me through to the demon king!"

I strode up to the group that was guarding her.

"Defend to the death, men! You're cleared to use magic!" another executive ordered, and in response, a volley of ice- and wind-blades flew at me.

The attack ripped my clothes just a little. I sustained some minor wounds.

But that was it.

"What, is that all? That was about like being bitten by a mosquito."

I saw dread run through them.

If this was all they had, they'd never be able to stop a level 99.

"If you get in my way, I'll take all of you down!"

I moved at high speed—and materialized right in front of the enemy.

"Good afternoon. For the sake of my personal convenience, take a nap, all right?"

I hit him with two punches in a row! And a kick!

This time, I used a Teleportation spell.

I appeared behind another one and hit him with a series of punches!

"There's no telling where the enemy will appear!" "She's too devastating!" "Somebody cast a Recovery spell!"

The demons were panicking. I was gonna keep this up.

I appeared behind them again, and this time I used a jump kick!

I sent one of them soaring.

I punched the guy next to him, too! One clean hit to the chin!

While I was at it, I got behind the one who was restraining Vania and kicked him in the back of the head! He dropped where he stood.

"You saved me, but Miss Azusa, what in the world is your status...?"

"What is it? Well, it's level ninety-nine."

I clobbered the remaining enemies in a similar fashion.

My opponents had no way to stop a strategy that combined teleportation with hand-to-hand combat. Leveling up over and over really was a shortcut to becoming the world's strongest.

I knocked down the soldiers who were guarding the demon king's room, armor and all.

In the end, I'd wiped out everyone except Beelzebub.

"I—I had no idea this would happen."

Beelzebub was petrified, too.

"If you got serious, you could raze an entire country by yourself..."

"I made a bigger show of it than was necessary. Still, I should be able to care for the demon king as much as I like now."

Taking my box of medicines, I entered the room where the demon king had to be.

The demon king, Provato Pecora Ariés, was asleep on a big canopy bed.

Great. Now if I manage to get the restorative medicine into her mouth, things should be all right.

I brought the medicine closer to the demon king's lips. I had to get her to open her mouth, so I'd need to touch her face a little...

In that instant, the demon king's eyes opened—and she butted me with her head.

Clonk.

I didn't dodge in time, and my head took damage.

Ow-ow-ow-ow... My defense was high, too, so the damage wasn't that bad, but even so.

"I sensed the approach of a miscreant, so my instincts roused me."

The demon king was already awake.

I see. Even if she's unconscious, she's able to detect enemies? That's a demon king for you.

...Wait.

If the demon king saw me as an enemy, wasn't that a bad thing? In multiple ways?

"Um, Your Majesty, I didn't come here to try to defeat you..."

"Azusa, Witch of the Highlands, fight me."

I had no idea where she'd taken it from, but the demon king drew a large sword.

Well, this got ugly fast.

"Your Majesty, I only brought a restorative medicine to wake you up. I have no intention of attacking you."

"But that green potion is obviously poisonous."

Frankly, you couldn't see it as anything but poison. I wouldn't want to drink it, either.

"You only think so, that's all. If you drank it, you'd start wanting to say, 'Oh, that's nasty! But give me another glass'!"

"I can't trust you! If you want me to believe you that badly, fight me, Provato Pecora Ariés, and prove your innocence!"

"H-how would that prove anything?"

"It's simple. If your goal is to harm my person, you'd never let me live. However, if you really intended to save me, you won't kill me, even if you win."

I see. That does make sense, in a way, but—

"But that only works if I win by a mile, doesn't it?"

"If you die, then you die. All that will remain is the fact that I killed an assassin."

She made her awful declaration without even blinking.

I could technically have refused to fight and made a run for it, but if I did, I'd completely lose my chance to explain myself. The situation could escalate into all-out war, and Beelzebub and Vania might be killed.

All right. I'd come to an internal conclusion.

We'd just have to let our fists do the talking.

Once more, I recalled my status.

AZUSA

Class: Witch | Level 99

HP : 533   MP : 867
ATK : 468   AGL : 841
DEF : 580   INT : 953

MAGIC
Teleportation, Levitation, Flame, Whirlwind,
Item Appraisal, Earthquake, Ice and Snow,
Lightning Attack, Mind Control, Break Spell,
Detoxify, Reflect Spell, Mana Absorption,
Language Comprehension, Transformation,
Spell Creation

SPECIAL ABILITIES, ETC.
Knowledge of medicinal herbs;
Immortality due to powers as a witch;
EXP acquisition boost.

EXPERIENCE POINTS
10,854,486

An ATK of 468, 580 DEF, and 533 HP. I should be more than capable in a hand-to-hand fight!

"All right, Witch of the Highlands. I'll judge your strength for you!"

I launched myself into a run, charging at the demon king, and she swung her enormous sword in a high-speed horizontal slash.

Foooooooooom! That was all she'd done, but it made a noise like a violent wind!

"Whoa!" For now, I shifted into an evasive maneuver, out of its path!

"What? You evaded that…? Your agility is incredible."

The demon king looked bewildered.

I would have expected no less of a demon king. Her abilities were definitely advanced. With all my previous enemies, I would have been able to dodge and then hit her without any trouble... Although I wasn't sure whether it would really be okay to do that.

I closed in one more time, but that sword really was dangerous.

She was swinging the blade around rapidly, apparently having studied the art.

I could have gotten in close anyway, but I didn't want to fight like a gambler, and I shouldn't. I wasn't allowed to lose. There were too many lives riding on me.

As befitted someone who called herself the demon king, my opponent was pretty powerful. If she swung that sword once, most opponents would die almost instantly.

That said, I wouldn't let her land blows that easily. My agility was at 841. If stats in this world could reach a maximum of 999, I was practically there.

That meant it wasn't easy to inflict damage on me.

I kept evading.

"Honestly! You keep scampering around! It looks like I'll manage to hit you, and then I don't!"

That's not it, demon king. I wasn't barely managing to evade at the last moment through luck. I was doing those split-second dodges because I could.

However, I had more to lose than my opponent did.

"If you take too long here, that elf's life will be in danger."

The demon king, who'd taken some distance, taunted me.

It was the wrong gibe to make. Those words set fire to my heart.

"Hurry and come at me, Witch of the Highlands!"

"I don't need you to tell me that."

To protect the lives of my family, I refused to compromise.

I sped up as fast as I could.

Then—I threw a punch that had all my strength behind it...

...at the demon king's sword.

Claaaaaaaaaaaaaaaaaang! A metallic sound went up from the blade

I'd hit. It sounded as if I'd struck it with another sword. So my hand was an actual weapon now?

Maybe it was because she'd taken the impact straight on, but the demon king staggered.

"Whoops…" She backed right into the wall, then stopped.

"I think that's the match, demon king."

"That call is premature. I lost my balance, but you aren't even close to cornering me."

"Ah. So you don't know yet."

I've always wanted to say that.

"Wh-what do you mean?!"

"I've already destroyed it, you see."

After a slight pause, the sword crumbled into fragments.

Stunned, the demon king dropped the now-useless sword.

"That can't possibly…"

"You can train your body as much as you like, but there are limits to how far weapons can be reinforced."

The sword had been in my way, so I'd gotten rid of it. That was the shortest route to saving Halkara.

Once I'd pulverized the weapon, it was my turn.

I sped up more.

I slammed my hand into the wall, right by the demon king's face.

Baaaaaaaaaaaaaaaaam!

It was a thoroughly ferocious smack that put cracks in the wall.

The demon king's expression finally warped.

"Yee…yeek…"

Apparently, she couldn't fight without her sword.

The way she was backing down would have been unthinkable if she could still fight.

"Checkmate, Your Majesty."

I kept the anger out of my face, smiling as much as I could. Still, I was taller, so I probably seemed pretty intimidating anyway.

"If we keep going, I'll win. Continuing isn't a good idea, is it?"

The demon king was looking up at my face through her lashes. The trembling might have been the reason she couldn't seem to get the words out.

"Will you listen to what I have to say?"

"Ah, ah…all right…"

"Spare Halkara please. She's just scatterbrained; she doesn't mean any harm. In addition, absolve of blame the demons who tried to help my family and me. It was all an unfortunate little mistake. If you say you'll forgive us, Your Majesty, everything will end well."

"………"

"Do you understand? That's important, so answer me properly. In words, please."

"Yes, my sister."

I get the feeling she just called me something odd.

—Just as I thought that, she put out a hand, reaching for my cheek. *Huh?! What's going on?! Can she use some sort of martial art after all?!* I couldn't sense anything that suggested she planned to kill me, though.

"I'll listen to whatever you say, my sister! I'm quite looking forward to it!"

"Um, what do you mean by your 'sister'?"

"I've often thought that I wanted someone stronger than myself to idolize. I suspected you might be perfect, Miss Azusa, so I tested you."

Tested? She intentionally picked a fight with me?!

"I would like to continue to love and respect you, Sister."

"Um, Your Majesty… I'd be honored to have your love and respect, but first, would you guarantee the safety of Halkara and the others? Also, could you remove your hand, please?"

"Oh no, don't speak so politely. Phrase it as an order: 'Provato, release my family,' like that. Ah, and also, lay your hand on my cheek, just as I'm doing now."

Finally, she retracted her hand.

I think this girl may have some rather odd proclivities…

Come to think of it, a long time ago, I read somewhere that the more powerful a person was, the more likely they were to be rather masochistic.

However, this was to save Halkara. There was no point in balking over giving an order.

"'Provato' isn't very cute. I'm calling you Pecora."

After all, her name was Provato Pecora Ariés. Although, with demons, I wasn't sure which was her first name and which was her family name.

"Yes, my sister."

Hiding my slight bewilderment, I put my right hand on Pecora's cheek.

"Oh, Sister…! What are you doing?"

In spite of what she said, she looked happy. Since I was doing exactly what she'd asked me to, that was probably only natural.

"Pecora, set Halkara free. I guarantee that she meant no harm, and well, ordinarily, they might execute her even so, but… If you say to retract it, then it can be retracted."

"All right, Sister. After all, I could never hurt my elder sister's friend."

Pecora (which was what I'd call her from now on) went out to where her executives were lying like piled-up corpses and told them, "Miss Azusa didn't intend to attack me. None of you is to consider her an enemy."

The executives who were still conscious prostrated themselves.

"In addition, though Miss Halkara head butted me, spare her. Miss Azusa's family must not be harmed."

A messenger demon was summoned immediately, and they went to where she was being detained to deliver the news.

Apparently, Halkara would be safe now. Good, that's a relief.

"It looks like it worked out one way or another."

Beelzebub gave a weary sigh.

"Oh! We're saved, too, then... I'm so glad..."

Vania had been tied up in coils and coils of rope. It had to have been quite a predicament, but she looked rather silly.

"A lot seems to have happened while I was unconscious. At a later date, I will conduct a review to see how the country functioned in my absence. For now, move ahead with the preparations for tomorrow's ceremony so that it can be held on schedule."

The demons nodded, then scattered in groups of twos and threes to do their jobs. She was calm, but I'd have expected no less from the demon king: Her dignity was in a league of its own.

"Oh. Your Majesty, could you also send word to my family that things have been safely resolved, please?"

"If you don't say it like my elder sister, I shan't listen," Pecora said primly.

"...Pecora, send word to my family, too. As quickly as possible."

"If it's an order from you, Sister, I'll have it done right away."

She'd listen to anything I said as long as I phrased it as an order, which was technically a good thing.

Haaaah... That's one job over with, and I'm tired.

When people's lives were on the line, it did make you tense. Even at level 99, your shoulders got stiff. *Maybe I'll take a little break.*

"Pecora, let's have tea. Tell them to prepare some for us."

"All right. We've made quite a mess of this place, so I'll have them get it ready in the building next door."

And so I had tea and waited with Demon King Pecora.

It might seem like a weird time for a tea party, but actually, this was the exact kind of situation that made me want to drink some tea and take it easy. I could see why the tea ceremony was popular during the Warring States era. When your body was fighting, your heart yearned for peace.

As an aside, on our way to the tea party venue, Pecora took my arm.

Apparently, she'd been looking for someone she could physically connect with on this level.

"I'm very happy to have found an elder sister. I'd grown weary of simply making everyone obey me."

"Isn't there anyone you can respect among the demons? A former teacher or someone like that?"

"When they see me, everyone naturally turns humble."

Well, after all, she was the king.

I could understand that. Sometimes, when people praised me too much as the Witch of the Highlands, it wore me out. Although, since Beelzebub treated me as an equal, it wasn't as bad as it could have been.

"What sort of tea would you like, my sister?"

"I don't know what kind you have, so you choose something, Pecora. Show me your good taste."

"That's a heavy responsibility…"

Pecora and I entered a sumptuous room, just the two of us.

The beverage her retainers brought in for us resembled a very spicy soup.

"What is this?"

"It's *nsuja* tea."

That was tough to pronounce. I wasn't sure, but it was probably a drink like butter tea. The demon lands were in the north, and I thought they probably needed a beverage that warmed them up. This one was pretty good, once you got used to it.

"Aah, tea with my elder sister. I've been looking forward to this day. I was right to choose you as a recipient for the Demon Medal… Although I never dreamed I'd lose consciousness."

Was it possible she'd called me here in order to form this mysterious pseudosister relationship with me?

"If there's any way the demons can be of service to you, just say the word, please. Your little sister will do everything she can for you."

So apparently, I now had the demons at my beck and call.

I'd acquired a strange level of authority before I really knew what was happening… Depending on how I used this, I could easily destroy a country.

Since she was calling me "elder sister," I thought it might be strange if I spoke to her too casually, so I tried talking a bit less and acting somewhat cool and distant. I also sharpened my gaze.

"Well, yes, I'll put you to work. Don't resent me for it, Pecora."

"Ooooh, nice. This is nice… An elder sister witch with a cool attitude. It doesn't get better than this…"

My act had been a smash hit?!

The demon king looked about ready to start drooling. Was she okay?

"When you pounded the wall beside me, Sister Azusa, it made my heart skip! A woman with a gallant expression giving me orders—I nearly swooned."

I'd unintentionally scored a direct hit on Pecora's preferences. I hadn't been acting, either; that had been serious.

"Um, Sister, I have a request."

"What, Pecora?"

"Would you kiss me on the cheek?"

"Huh?"

I felt as if she'd just said something weird to me.

"In my favorite book, there's a scene where the older sister kisses her sworn younger sister on the cheek, and I just love it. I've truly longed for something like that."

Pecora had flushed red, and she put her hands to her face.

"And, you see, no one's here right now..."

True, the retainers who'd brought in the tea had all gone away again.

"You kiss family members, don't you? This is merely an extension of that."

Was it like that among the demons? In some countries, I'd heard it was pretty common to do that to your family, but I'd never done it to mine... It would have been easy to do it to my daughters, but if I had, I most likely wouldn't have been able to stop there and would have had to include Laika and Halkara as well, so I'd kept it to hugs.

"All right. Only on the cheek, though."

If no one was looking anyway, it was fine. Besides, right now, it would be dangerous to treat Pecora badly.

"Th-thank you very much, Sister!"

It was just a little peck on the cheek. There was no need to be so nervous about it. It had nothing to do with romance, either.

I got up from my chair and put my face near Pecora's cheek.

"Close your eyes, Pecora."

Pecora obeyed my order.

If I kept her in suspense for too long, I'd freeze up as well, so I immediately moved my lips closer.

Just then, the door opened.

"My, but that was frightening, Madam Teacher. They very nearly put me in a flooded chamber."

Halkara had come in.

But of course, at the moment, I was just about to kiss Pecora, and...

The kiss was interrupted, but Halkara had already seen more than enough.

"Wha... Madam Teacher, you and the demon king are... Wh— Wha— Whaaaaaaaaaaat?!"

She was clearly about to blow a fuse.

"Calm down, Halkara! Actually, that's an order. Settle down!"

"Madam Teacher, are you the type who falls for women?! I see... I, um... You have my support."

"I don't particularly need your support!"

"Only, if that's the case, it does put me in an awkward position. We live in the same house, and you've never made a single move on me... Am I that unattractive? I feel a strange sense of failure..."

"You haven't lost at anything! You don't have to feel miserable, all right?!"

While I was explaining myself, Pecora was looking miffed.

Her face was redder than I'd ever seen it.

"You! Barging in on my precious time with my elder sister—have you no delicacy?! That's one thing I absolutely shan't forgive! I'll have you executed!"

Whaaaaaaaaaaat?!

"First you release me, and now you're having me killed?! Spare me, I'm begging you! I'll do anything, so please forgive me!"

Halkara despaired; she was on the verge of tears.

"You can't execute her! Forgive her! Okay?! Please?!"

"Don't stop me, Sister! That woman spoiled my fantasy!"

"No, I'm stopping you! I can't not stop you!"

Hmm… How can I put her in a better mood?

"In that case, would you like me to kiss you now?"

"No. The atmosphere's been ruined. Kisses are a ritual to deepen the bonds between older and younger sisters. They're more than a mere brush of the lips."

Apparently, she was very picky about these things.

In the end, I no longer had to kiss anybody, I managed to soothe Pecora somehow, and Halkara was forgiven.

After that, my family was safely reunited.

When Halkara returned to the room, Falfa jumped on her. Shalsha and Laika sighed with relief.

"For a while, I really wasn't sure what would happen. Halkara, please do live just a little more cautiously."

"I worried you, too, didn't I, Laika? I'm very sorry."

This time, Halkara seemed to be doing some serious soul-searching.

"Still, all's well that ends well. Welcome back. Take your time—relax and rest today."

Laika's expression grew gentle. Everyone had been anxious about Halkara.

"Thank you very much. A little later, and they would have begun to torture me…"

"By the way, where is Rosalie? I don't see her."

Rosalie's face emerged from the wall right beside me.

"Oh, sorry, I was in the wall!"

"Waugh! You scared me!"

I flinched. It was bad enough that I jumped and almost stepped on Halkara's foot.

Still, we really were all together now.

Suddenly, I began to want to do a certain something to my daughters.

If an action isn't wrong, it's best to go right ahead and do it.

First, I called to Shalsha, who was nearby.

"Shalsha, come here a moment, please."

Shalsha trotted over.

I scooped her up in a hug and planted a kiss on her cheek.

"Oh! A kiss…"

Even after I put Shalsha down, she seemed dazed for a little while.

"I've decided I'll kiss you two from now on… That's all right, isn't it? I know I'm asking after the fact, but…"

Pecora had inspired me, and I'd decided to kiss my daughters as their mother.

Our relationship was more nebulous than the one a normal parent and her children would have had in the first place, so it was important for us to confirm that we were family this way.

"…I don't mind at all."

Maybe it was embarrassing; Shalsha's face had flushed a little.

"Mommy! Falfa too! Falfa too!"

Falfa was bouncing up and down. *Of course I'll kiss you.*

It was my policy to treat both my daughters equally. Even if their personalities were different, there really mustn't be any inequality in the love I showered them with. After all, if I hadn't killed slimes, neither of them would have been born.

Falfa leaped at me, and I caught her in a hug. Then I kissed her.

They were both slime spirits, but their cheeks weren't as springy as slimes— Well, but they were incredibly resilient. Was this the phenomenon known as "youth"? Or was it really because they were slimes?

"Yaaaay! Mommy kissed me!"

Falfa was delighted, without a trace of embarrassment. *That's right. Between parents and children, no embarrassment is necessary.*

"Mommy, Falfa wants to kiss you, too!"

"Sure. Wait just a minute, though."

I wanted to be as equal as possible, respecting both their wills...

"Do you want to kiss your mother, too, Shalsha?"

Shalsha nodded. "Uh-huh."

"In that case, kiss me from both sides."

In perfect sync, my daughters kissed me on the cheeks.

Having your daughters kiss you. For a mother, was there any time when real life felt more fulfilling? It was probably safe to say no. I'd worked very hard, so it was okay for me to have a perk like this, wasn't it?

"All right, you two. Thank you."

"I think Falfa likes you even more now, Mommy!"

"It isn't possible to express love in quantitative terms like 'more' or 'less.'"

At times like this, their differences became apparent.

I'd have to thank Demon King Pecora for teaching me about the notion of kisses.

"My, my. Kisses between parents and children are nice as well, aren't they?"

I heard a voice I'd just been listening to a little while ago.

When I turned, Pecora had opened the door and come in.

Involuntarily, Halkara braced herself. True, she had very nearly ended up in a dangerous situation.

Laika had braced herself as well, but in a different way. Halkara had prepared to run, while Laika seemed ready to fight.

"Pecora, what...?"

"I heard that none of you had eaten yet. Since we had the opportunity, I thought we might be able to eat together."

I see. That wasn't a bad idea. Actually, when I heard the word *eat*, I realized that I was incredibly hungry.

Well, of course. Until I was sure everybody was safe, food had been out of the question. Human bodies were apparently pretty tactful about things like that.

"Perfect timing. Where should we go?"

"I'll show you to the dining room for guests. Come, Sister, let us go."

Pecora took my arm, as if it was the most natural thing in the world.

I got the feeling that, of the people I'd met so far, this girl spoke the most with her actions. Falfa was my daughter, so she got special treatment.

"Oh… Lady Azusa…"

Laika looked a little lonely. True, she was just my apprentice, so she walked a step behind. When this is all over, perhaps I should dote on her a bit more.

"It's like Madam Teacher has been taken away, and I feel almost defeated after all."

Halkara felt something similar, apparently. Managing distance in relationships was unexpectedly hard… That was a problem for later.

"Listen, Pecora, don't you think you're being too clingy?"

However, Pecora paid no attention to what I'd said; she clutched my arm even more tightly.

"This is what pseudosister relationships are like. Please play along with my fantasy, just for a little while, elder sister."

Well, there hadn't been anyone to fill the role of big sister to the demon king, so there might be no way out of this. She'd probably been lonely.

"Yes, all right. I did promise I would."

I stroked Pecora's head. I wasn't sure if it would be a faux pas to pet her ovine horns, so I didn't touch them.

"Aaaah, I got knocked out today, but this happiness is enough to cancel all that."

I was honored by her utter lack of embarrassment as she shared her joy with me.

"Um, Sister, could I ask you to carry me to the dining room in your arms, like a princess?"

"You're pretty demanding, aren't you?"

"Well, I am the demon king, after all. Of course I'm willful."

True, she didn't seem apologetic, but she took no petty delight in controlling other people, either. In her life, it was simply her place to ask others for things.

"Besides, I suppose I might call it a replacement for that kiss that didn't happen. Sisters should have special moments like those."

"That's true. Is this how you want me to carry you?"

I picked Pecora up. Possibly because I was level 99, I didn't lose my balance or drop her.

"In the arms of my elder sister... Those scenes that I fantasized about from the story really are wonderful..."

Laika and Halkara followed us. They didn't look as if they were enjoying themselves much.

"Halkara, I believe I may not be terribly fond of that person."

"If I had to say, I can't deal with her, either. I think sheltered rich girls like her would grow better if they experienced some of the harshness the world has to offer. For example, maybe she should work at my factory, with an additional eighty hours of overtime a month."

I think that was probably a joke, but don't you dare give your employees that much overtime.

I had no idea that Pecora would irritate those two so much... I'd better smooth things over somehow. I preferred not to rock the boat.

"Oh! You just thought of something besides me, didn't you, Sister?"

Pecora puffed out her cheeks a bit.

"I'm free to think whatever I like, aren't I?"

"When you're carrying your little sister in your arms, though, it's only natural to think of her."

So apparently, the princess carry was bound by a variety of rules, too.

"Come, don't you have anything to say about this? 'You're very light, you know,' or something like that."

"Maybe it's your fancy clothes, but you're beginning to feel heavier and heavier."

"You're so mean, Sister."

Pecora puffed out her cheeks crossly again, but—

"I like being toyed with by my mean elder sister, too."

In the end, she looked happy.

On the way, the other demons watched us, looking terribly taken aback, but no one said anything.

I guess there isn't a demon anywhere who can complain to their king.

Beelzebub and Vania were waiting outside the dining room.

Beelzebub looked a little—or rather, very—disgusted.

"Your Majesty, don't you think you're overdoing it a bit?"

"Well, there's no one in this world who's fit to acknowledge as my elder sister. I'd thought that you might be a big-sister candidate, Beelzebub, but you've never scolded me even once."

Pecora pouted. She seemed to be quite a spirited girl.

Beelzebub and the rest probably had a pretty hard time here.

"Haaa… Azusa, play the big sister properly, would you? The job's too much for me."

"All right. I'll handle it for the next few days."

"If possible, I'd like you to come here once every couple of months."

Was this strange relationship going to go on forever? I might have roped myself into something awkward…

"I know! Why don't you eat with us, Beelzebub? Your subordinate is welcome, too."

Our group now consisted of the usual suspects for parties at my house, plus Pecora and Vania. Well, it was nice to have things lively.

The demons' court cuisine was all highly seasoned, but it was delicious. I was glad we hadn't been served insects or something.

During the meal, Pecora spoke to me again and again: "Sister, is there any type of liquor you'd like to drink?" "Sister, do tell me if there are any dishes you fancy." "Sister, Sister."

"Why don't you act a little more like a demon king?"

"That would be boring, no different from what I usually do. I want to do all I can for you, as your little sister."

I had the authority to make the demon king do anything I wanted. *How should I use this…?*

"Later on, could you teach me a few things about the plants that grow in the demon lands? I might be able to develop new medicines based on them."

"Of course! I'll make the arrangements right away!"

This would benefit my home area, too, so I'd call it a win.

"Tomorrow is finally the day of the medal conferment. I can't wait!"

"Come to think of it, that is why we're actually here, isn't it?"

I wondered what sort of event it would end up being.

"Oh, that's right... Laika, wasn't it?"

Unusually, Pecora said a name that wasn't mine.

"Yes, Your Majesty. What is it?"

Since Pecora was clinging to me, Laika still looked nonplussed.

"Tomorrow, you'll be reunited with someone unexpected."

"Pardon?"

Instead of answering, Pecora just smiled mischievously.

The next day, we put on our dresses and went to the ceremony venue.

Despite the eventful day before, the site of the ceremony was decorated with flowers as though nothing had happened at all. My rampage probably wouldn't be made public.

There were other people who didn't seem to be demons, besides us. From what I overheard of their conversations, they were scholars. Evidently, it was true that the demons held this ceremony to honor all sorts of people.

"I'm nervous, but this is hard for other reasons."

People I'd fought yesterday were here as well. We greeted one another awkwardly: "I apologize for my rudeness yesterday." "No, no, I should be saying that to you..."

As a result, when I spotted Beelzebub and Vania, I felt a little relieved.

"For a while there, I really wasn't sure what was going to happen."

"I could say the same. That was the biggest crisis I've ever had, too…
I thought things wouldn't get boring if I was with you, but I'd really
rather not have any more of this, thank you."

Beelzebub still looked worn out.

I could tell from the way her wings were fluttering. On top of that,
even though it wasn't hot, she was waving her feathered fan.

"I thought I might die, too. Actually, I was already prepared for it."

Vania also looked rather haggard.

Beside Vania was another demon whose face strongly resembled hers.

"Who's this?"

"I'm the leviathan Fatla. I was the one you rode here."

"Oh! Thank you very much!"

"I'm acting as a staff member at today's ceremony. Personally, flying
is a lot easier for me. You know how it is; entertaining guests takes a lot
of emotional energy."

I knew what she meant. Back when I was chained to my company,
chauffeuring had been easier than taking care of guests.

"Well, I'm looking forward to serving you today. Please enjoy a drink
before the ceremony."

Fatla offered us glasses with something alcoholic in them. This might
have been a universal custom.

Laika took a glass after I did. However, at that point, Vania broke in.

"Um, listen… If anyone here gets intoxicated easily or doesn't handle alcohol well, drink water instead, okay?"

Vania's eyes were clearly on Halkara.

"All right. I'll be cautious."

Since Halkara was being careful, we probably wouldn't have trouble
this time.

"Falfa and Shalsha, you have water, too."

Slimes apparently weren't good at breaking down alcohol. Since this
fact fit their childlike appearances, it was easy to understand in a way.

"Since this is a demon ceremony, I wondered what it would be like,
but it's quite sophisticated, isn't it, Lady Azusa?"

Laika was gazing around at the venue, looking very much like a well-bred young lady.

"You're used to ceremonies, aren't you, Laika? I suppose you would be."

"Yes. This isn't much different from dragon ceremonies. I imagine the proceedings will end without trouble."

Laika, comments like that tend to jinx things, so I really wish you wouldn't.

Just then, the soldiers loudly called: "Presenting Her Majesty the demon king!"

Pecora appeared on a slightly raised dais.

"Ladies and gentlemen, thank you for taking time out of your busy schedules to attend today. I am the demon king, Provato Pecora Ariés. I'll get straight to business and award the Demon Medals in order. First, the magic division. Mr. Mantoya, for vastly improving the level of defense reinforcement magic."

Pecora handed something that appeared to be a medal to a man who was very obviously a magician.

This part went the way you'd expect it to as well.

"Next, the nature division. Mr. Noreil, who has successfully culti-vated blue roses."

The next individual to appear was an elderly man who seemed to have no idea why he'd been summoned to such a place. It was easy to imagine that the demons had suddenly informed him that they were awarding him a medal and told him to show up.

After that, she went on to recognize various divisions.

It was probably due to Pecora's temperament, but the ceremony itself felt casual, and it wasn't tedious.

"All right, next is the peace division. Miss Azusa, the Witch of the Highlands, if you would."

Accompanied by applause, I went to stand in front of the dais. I'd been through quite a lot just to receive this medal.

However, at that point, Pecora smiled mischievously.

Argh, that expression... She's gotta be plotting something.

"As a matter of fact, it isn't just Miss Azusa."

"What do you mean?"

"You put an end to the long feud between the red and blue dragons. Since we have this opportunity, I'd like to award medals to the dragons as well."

Pecora's eyes went to Laika.

"Huh? Me too?"

Laika pointed to her own face. Applause broke out, and so she had to come up on the dais as well.

"I see. This is a rather nice idea," I said.

It was true that, without Laika's help, I wouldn't have been able to stop the fight. However, if this was all, then Pecora's expression didn't make sense...

"Well, Miss Laika the red dragon is here. Let's have a representative from the blue dragons as well. Miss Flatorte, come to the front, please!"

""Huh?!""

Laika and I yelped in unison.

A girl with horns and a dragon tail opened the door and came in.

There was no mistake. It was Flatorte in her human form.

Earlier, she had been the leader of the blue dragons who'd forced their way into Laika's big sister's wedding. We'd trounced her completely, and she'd been forced into a nonaggression pact with the red dragons.

"Miss Flatorte is in charge of the blue dragons, after all, and she's making sure that no more fights occur. I thought she should receive a medal, too."

"You do like surprising people, don't you?"

Timidly, Flatorte came up onto the dais as well.

As you'd expect, she didn't seem comfortable standing beside Laika... Although the reverse was also true.

"I-it's been a long time, Laika…"

"Yes, it has. I'm glad we've stopped meeting each other on battlefields."

"All right, I'm conferring a medal to each of you."

Pecora was rather sloppy as she hung the medals on each of them.

"Now the dragons' peace is even more secure. I can't imagine anyone would start a fight."

Pecora smiled brightly. It was the "If you violate this, the demons will fly into a rage and attack you" system.

"I—I know…that. The blue dragons won't do anything, so…"

Flatorte was trembling rather noticeably. Even dragons were scared of the demon king.

"Pecora, you may not seem to be the meticulous type, but that was a pretty clever idea."

"As the demon king, I must ensure that the world stays in line." Pecora looked quite proud of herself. "In the coming age, the demon king will become a symbol of racial cooperation. After all, our nation is home to a vast number of ethnic groups."

True, even if you called them all "demons," physically, they were awfully diverse. Maybe that made them tolerant?

"Well, I believe I'll take my leave now… I still have all sorts of errands to run…"

Flatorte was already eager to make her escape. Being here had to be awkward for her. Besides, while it might have been different if she'd won, she'd lost to her intended victims.

However, I didn't miss the way Pecora smirked again for a moment.

I was beginning to understand her. Pecora had an extremely bad personality. Not only that, but she was aware of it, which made it incredibly hard to deal with.

"I just had a thought. I'd like to have you prove the blue dragons' continued obedience to my elder sister as well."

Was she going to make me do something again?

"Sister, stroke Miss Flatorte's horns, if you would. I hear that the blue dragons let individuals to whom they show absolute obedience pet their horns."

Pecora beamed. It was an adorable smile, but it contained a subtle hint of sadism.

"Eeeeep! N-no, not the horns… Not the horns…"

Flatorte was backing away.

Laika was watching Flatorte sympathetically. "The demon king shows no mercy, does she?"

"Is having someone touch your horns really such a bad thing?"

"It's a custom peculiar to the blue dragons, and it signifies total submission. If they break the rule against it, death becomes their only alternative—and so, in battles up till now, the red dragons have always been careful not to touch them there."

I didn't have horns myself, so I didn't quite understand the feelings here.

"It's said that long ago, when adventurers tried to touch dragons' horns to make them their own, many of them lost their lives. For the most part, they were hit with their cold breath and perished before they touched them."

I see. I'd heard stories of knights who rode dragons—so those had been blue dragons?

"If Laika, who is a red dragon, touched them, it would put the blue dragons under the complete control of the red dragons, and I expect that would be awkward for you two. That means that having the Witch of the Highlands touch them is perfect. In other words, we'll add an additional fetter to the existing ones."

Pecora really was a schemer.

Granted, that might have been precisely why she was succeeding as the demon king, but…

"Well, it is for the sake of peace. I guess I will touch them."

"D-do whatever you want… Argh, I don't even care anymore…"

Flatorte wilted and hung her head.

In that case, I'll touch those horns.

I put out my hand and stroked the horns. Pet-pet, pet-pet. They were hard, like stone.

"My ancestors... Flatorte has submitted to the witch. I beg your forgiveness for bringing shame upon you..."

It was brutal of Pecora to do something like this in public, I thought, and I stopped.

"Well done. That ends the commendation ceremony. You may repair to the buffet party."

And now my job at the ceremony was over.

However, I still had one strange problem: Flatorte kept following me around.

Even when I went to go fill my plate from the various dishes, she was right behind me. I thought the only people who'd stick that close were assassins or attendants. Was this some new form of harassment?

"Um, what did you need?"

"I—I am...now under the control of the great Witch of the Highlands, so...I am staying behind you, in case you need me."

I had a very bad feeling about this.

"When does this 'control' business end? Tomorrow? Three days from now?"

"When I die."

Yes, that bad feeling had been right on the mark!

"So you're going to follow me back home?!"

"That's correct..."

The whole time Flatorte spoke, her face was red with humiliation. Since she looked like a girl, I felt as if I was doing something pretty awful.

Meanwhile, Laika seemed to think that this was a nuisance.

"Lady Azusa, the house in the highlands does not need two dragons. I-I'm enough. Order Flatorte to return to the blue dragons' hometown. If she owes you absolute obedience and you tell her to go home, she will."

Laika was right.

It would be mean to force her to move house, and all I had to do was "order" her to live at home, the way she'd always done.

"According to the customs of the blue dragons, when we part from the one who controls us, we must end our lives. After all, it is our duty to protect that person forever…"

"That's one harsh custom!"

Pecora was a short distance away, and our eyes met.

Her face seemed to say, Sister, do take care of that Flatorte person, won't you?

"Pecora knew all that, and she still had me touch you! She has a sweet face, but she's a little demon!"

"Lady Azusa, she is their king, a demon among demons," Laika pointed out.

"You're right… Demons really are scary…"

That was when Beelzebub strode up to us and immediately bowed her head.

"Her Majesty is quite fond of pranks… She isn't a bad person, and she's very clever, but sometimes she does odd things on impulse. I'm sorry."

"Well, it's not as if it's caused me serious trouble. It's all right."

With Demon King Pecora as the benchmark, Beelzebub looked like a careworn middle manager.

"Um…I'll do anything, so please take me with you."

Flatorte kept her head lowered the whole time, gazing at the ground.

"Yes, yes, it's fine, just raise your head."

"Yes, Mistress Witch of the Highlands."

If she was in her human form, it wouldn't be a problem if we had her live in one of the empty rooms.

"It looks like you've been roped into something awful, but we'll take you in, so don't worry. Besides, no one will blame you for coming to where I am. We'll visit your hometown once in a while, too."

"Thank you very much, mistress!"

She knelt on the spot.

Somehow, I'd gotten fearsomely important, or so it felt, and it was really awkward.

"You're lucky the merciful Lady Azusa was the one to pick you up."

Maybe Laika wasn't really all that displeased about having another dragon around.

"Laika, I won't lose to you!"

However, Flatorte abruptly raised her head.

"Wh-what do you mean?!"

"I will submit to my mistress, but that is all! I won't submit to you!"

"I have seniority here! You're being rude!"

"It doesn't matter who's new and who has seniority! You aren't my mistress!"

The two of them snarled at each other and began to fight.

I bet this is going to get complicated...

Our tour of Vanzeld Castle hadn't exactly been without mishap, but it had ended without any actual injuries.

I'd wanted to do a little more sightseeing, but the number of people who'd be living at the house in the highlands had increased, and we'd decided to head straight back.

At present, we were on our way home aboard a leviathan.

While we were relaxing in the dining area, a demon came in.

"I'll be your attendant on your return journey, Fatla. My little sister, Vania, caused all manner of trouble for you during the first half of your voyage."

Oh, that's right. These sisters took their huge leviathan forms in turns and worked as something resembling a sightseeing bus. The one who wasn't driving (?) acted as the tour conductor.

"No, no. Vania was trying her best, I think. Don't worry about it."

"Are you sure? From what I can see, she's practically dead weight for our tribe."

When it came to her little sister, she had a very sharp tongue.

"I'll guide you properly, so please don't worry. I've prepared beverages for you as well, and I'll go get them now."

After about three minutes, Fatla came back with a tray of chilled drinks.

"It's a beverage made by dissolving honey in spring water. It should be just the thing for the fatigue of a long journey."

"You really are good at hospitality."

If Demon King Pecora had had a slightly better personality and we had managed to stay out of trouble, this probably would have been an ordinary trip... Although I guess you could say it was typical of us to get dragged into something like this. It wasn't easy living a laid-back life.

But there was still an accident waiting for us.

Abruptly, the floor pitched and rolled.

"An earthquake? But we aren't even on the ground!!"

"Vania probably made herself laugh by remembering something, and she's shaking! That idiot!"

I see. If you don't stay calm, anybody and anything you're carrying will rock, too.

Then the pitching grew more violent, and...

"Waugh, argh! She's moving so much I can't balance the tray—"

Fatla toppled over.

Sploosh! The honey-water on the tray splashed all over her.

"I-I'm not a klutz! I'm not!"

Fatla had landed on her rear, and tears were welling in her eyes.

"Lady Beelzebub always praised me, saying I did my job well... This is abominable! I swear, I'm going to give Vania such a beating later!!!"

"Hey, calm down! Does anybody have a towel?"

Halkara went and got one, and we dried Fatla off a little.

While we were toweling her down, an announcement echoed through the room.

"This is your pilot, Vania. I'm very sorry about that. A joke from a comedy I saw two years ago just popped into my head..."

So she actually had laughed because she'd remembered something?!

"I am never ever ever forgiving you!"

Fatla was beside herself with fury.

Well, this was a family problem, and I'd let them work it out on their own.

Fifteen minutes later, Fatla brought in some fresh honey-water. Her expression was composed.

She was warm with a vague glow about her, as if she'd just gotten out of the bath.

"I was sticky from the honey, so I washed off and soaked a little. Here are some fresh beverages for you."

"You have it pretty rough, don't you?"

"Yes, it's truly awful."

The honey-water wasn't too sweet. The flavor was perfectly balanced.

As you drank it, it made you feel as though your body was being quietly purified.

My daughters were offering comments like, "This is good, isn't it, Shalsha?!" "Yes, Sister, it's delicious," so by all appearances, it was a hit with the children as well.

"Bring me another glass, please." Halkara ordered seconds. "If we commercialized this, I think it would sell quite nicely. If it's simply water and honey, it should be easy enough to prepare. I'll drink a little more and memorize the flavor."

"You're incredibly business-minded!"

"I caused trouble for you again, so I thought I'd earn money and get a present for everyone…"

Between this and that, Halkara also seemed to be reflecting on her actions.

"Halkara, you don't need to show your consideration that way." As Laika spoke, she sipped her honey-water. "On the contrary, I believe Lady Azusa wants you to use this error to help yourself grow. If you wish to repay us with something concrete, simply treat us to elvish cuisine at the house in the highlands."

Rosalie, who was floating beside her, also nodded. I agreed.

"All right. Thank you very much… Still, this does seem as if it would sell, so I'll keep the honey-water product in mind."

So she hadn't forgotten the business aspect. In a way, that was just like Halkara. Thinking that I wanted her to keep living life her way, I drank down the last of my honey-water.

However, there was still one glass sitting on the table, completely untouched.

"Flatorte, why aren't you drinking? Don't you like it?"

Flatorte was going back to the house in the highlands as well, and she was right there with us. However, for the past little while, she hadn't said a word, and she hadn't drunk or eaten anything.

"Is this some sort of protest?"

Could it be a hunger strike?

"No." Flatorte shook her head, but she was gazing at the honey-water. "You didn't give me permission to drink, mistress, so I haven't."

She gave the rather shocking reason very casually.

Halkara, Laika, and Rosalie all recoiled a bit.

"…You may drink, Flatorte."

When I gave permission, Flatorte took a normal sip and smiled. "It's delicious."

Was the girl a fanatic, or was the blue dragons' submission extreme? Either way, this wasn't good.

"Flatorte, come here a minute."

I took the dragon into an empty room.

"Whatever's the matter, mistress? Have I done something wrong?"

"Listen, does this mean that you won't—or can't—do anything unless you're ordered to?"

"That is the way master-servant relationships are, so yes. There was a time, long ago, when human knights fought astride blue dragons. Back then, if a dragon acted without orders, it would cause a huge incident, and so…"

I see. So the submission was based on a wartime mentality.

"In that case, if I told you to die, would you do it? That's not right, is it?"

"If you tell me to die, I will. That is the pride of the blue dragons."

This was a problem. I was currently clashing with a values system that was different from mine.

"Flatorte, you don't want to die, do you?"

"N-no, I don't, but as a blue dragon, there are things I must protect…"

"Dying when someone tells you to die is pride? But you're just throwing yourself away. I know submission isn't the only thing your people consider a virtue."

Somehow, I'd have to shift Flatorte's mindset into something more decent.

"No. The blue dragons' core value is that 'the strong take everything.' In other words…it follows that a defeated individual who's allowed their horns to be touched must live out the rest of their days in absolute obedience to the stronger party."

As Flatorte told me this, there were tears in her eyes. She hadn't fully accepted the unfairness of the situation, either.

"My parents taught me this as well. The type who would let their horns be touched should lose everything and live on that way. They said it was the punishment for being weak."

"But that's practically slavery."

"In the ancient manuscripts, I hear that dragon knights are defined as 'those who fight by using enslaved blue dragons.'"

Hey, no, I don't want a slave. We're already living pretty happily as a family.

"All right. In that case, Flatorte, I have an order for you."

"Yes, mistress."

"Once we reach the house in the highlands, think and act on your own, without waiting for orders from me. Throw away the sense of submission and live any way you like."

Flatorte didn't seem to understand what she'd just heard, but soon her expression turned anxious.

"But mistress, in that case, I won't know how I should live!"

"Why not? My orders are absolute, aren't they? In that case, obey them. You have to live independently. I'll give you as much advice as you like, but I'm not fond of giving orders."

Flatorte was gazing at me with tear-filled eyes.

Apparently, what I was trying to say had gotten through to her a little.

"Mistress, that order is inconsistent..."

Right: There was something twisted about being *ordered* to act *freely*.

"That's fine. After all, I'm the one in charge around here."

When I think something is right, I don't back down.

"You really are kind, aren't you, mistress?"

"If anything, you're too extreme. Take life a bit easier. In a way, if you tried to emulate Halkara, it would be just about perfect."

"Mistress, in that case... May I ask a favor?"

"I'll do what I can. What is it?"

"Would you pet my horns and head, please?"

Huh? Horn-petting again?

"There's no real harm in it, so I suppose it's fine."

I thumped Flatorte's back lightly with my left hand, petting her horns and head with my right.

"Aah... Flatorte is yours, mistress..."

Flatorte sounded happy. Was it safe to consider this matter settled?

"Among the blue dragons, I was always careful not to show weakness...so there was no one I could ask to spoil me, and so...I'm very happy right now."

Come to think of it, this girl had been the leader during that attack.

Like Pecora, she might fall into the "many important people are masochists" category.

"Mistress, Mama, Mama..."

"Huh? Mama?"

True, mothers were the ultimate example of people you could count on to spoil you, but...

This was just a guess, but maybe when your parents stroked your horns, it didn't count as far as submission was concerned. Parents probably at least petted their children's heads.

In that case, the only people who could pet your horns would be your master or your parents. It had probably made her remember her mother.

"It feels nice in your tummy, Mama... It's like when I'm lying down in a warm room..."

It did seem as though her memories were reverting to early childhood. Was she regressing because she sensed something maternal in me—even though I was younger than she was—and wanted me to spoil her? I was in full mommy mode toward this adorable dragon already, so I wasn't picking up on the finer points of Flatorte's emotions.

At this stage, I might be able to raise one more rather odd child.

Just then, the door to the room opened, and Laika came in. Her face was pretty stern.

She yanked on Flatorte's back.

"You're causing trouble for Lady Azusa. I think it's about time you removed yourself!"

Flatorte was pulled away easily. However, when she saw Laika, her fury blazed up. Her regression to infancy evaporated.

"Why did you interrupt us?! Every last thing red dragons do is irritating!"

"You were doing something strange, so I stopped you, that's all!"

"It looks as though I really will have to settle things with you somewhere! I challenge you to a duel!"

So what exactly had they sworn in the presence of the demon king again?! They'd already gone back to fighting?!

"Don't, you two! If you make the demon king look bad, terrible things will happen!"

"Mistress, if we challenge each other in a way that isn't recognizable as fighting, there won't be a problem."

"Lady Azusa, I believe it will be all right if we choose a safe method."

That was a relief. In that case, though, what on earth were they planning to do?

"Wh-what about whoever serves mistress best wins…?"

What was that method supposed to be?!

"A-all right… That will do."

Not only that, but Laika accepted it!

"M-mistress? Are your shoulders stiff?"

"Lady Azusa, I'll massage your back."

"No, both places are fine already!"

I left the room. Having people come at me with that extraordinary resolve only makes my shoulders stiffen up more!

"Once we reach the house in the highlands, we'll have a cooking competition!"

"Perfect. I'll make sweets mistress will find delicious!"

I guess the house is going to get even noisier.

"Excuse me, I brought somebody home with me."

When Halkara returned from the factory, she was holding a leopard-spotted kitten in her arms.

...Or was it indeed a young leopard?

In any case, it was definitely a feline.

"I saw this little guy near the factory. He was all alone, and he looked cold. And then, when I held out my hand, he just got so attached to me... He's saying, 'I want mew to adopt me,' isn't he?"

Halkara was smiling cheerfully, but the kitten was gnawing on her hand. *Doesn't that hurt...?*

"That animal is a Nanterre wildcat. Ordinarily, they live in deserted places; it may have wandered into town by accident, or possibly its mother abandoned it," Laika, who took Halkara to and from work, explained. As she spoke, she was watching Halkara get bitten. "As a rule, the species doesn't domesticate well, so—"

"But look, he's taken such a liking to me! I don't think any animal has ever loved me this much!"

Halkara cut Laika off firmly.

"Madam Teacher, I'm keeping this little one! I'll be his mother!"

Frankly speaking, it was hard to believe Halkara could take care of an animal. Besides, at this point, it didn't seem to like her at all.

"He says so, too. 'I want an elf to take care of me.'"

"Halkara, you keep saying 'he,' but I believe the kitten is a girl."

"M-maybe she's a tomboy! It's fine!"

At that point, Falfa and Shalsha came to see what was going on.

"Ooh, cutie, how cute! It's a kitty!"

Falfa's energy levels hit the ceiling.

The kitten jumped out of Halkara's arms and went over to her.

"Kitty, good girl, good girl. ♪"

When Falfa petted her head, the kitten purred. She didn't look as if she was planning to bite my daughter. Shalsha also gingerly petted the kitten from the side.

Aww… *My Daughters, Featuring Kitten*. It was the cutest thing in the universe!

"Shalsha thinks we could probably take care of her at this size."

"Falfa wants to keep the kitty! Can we, Mommy?"

"Shalsha is interested in observing animals as well."

"Sure. As a matter of fact, we have to keep her."

The kitten brought out my daughters' cuteness, and so she was staying here. Maybe I really should study magic, make a camera, and take photos of my daughters and the cat.

"Good work, Halkara. I appreciate your initiative."

"Madam Teacher, did Falfa's reaction just drastically change your evaluation?"

Halkara wore a rather complicated expression.

The kitten—strictly speaking, she may not have been a cat, but she was pretty similar—was named Doughnut.

This happened because she was the exact same color as the doughnuts we'd made two days earlier.

Halkara was the one who gave her the name. She was the one who'd brought her home, so she got to name her.

It seemed overly simplistic to me, but it was true that a unique name would probably have been harder to remember, so that was okay.

At first, maybe because Doughnut wasn't used to being indoors, she prowled around exploring everything. However, at some point, she began going up to a certain person.

"This cat can see me..."

Doughnut gazed steadily at Rosalie. Apparently, cats could see ghosts.

It seemed as though Doughnut had two or three set Rosalie-viewing times each day.

Come to think of it, a cat that had belonged to one of my high school friends would sometimes stare out the window at certain times. When the translucent paper windows were closed, it would meow, demanding that we slide them open.

By the way, all you could see out the window of my friend's house were concrete blocks; there hadn't even been any potted plants. The feline aesthetic sense was an enigma.

However, you couldn't really say that Doughnut had taken a liking to Rosalie. The one she was friendliest with was Falfa, or maybe Halkara. It all depended on what you took into consideration when making your decision. It was a bit like the way committee members' evaluations differed widely when they decided who to award with the literary Akutagawa Prize.

"Doughnut, din-din time. ♪"

When Falfa set out a saucer of milk, Doughnut darted right over. She seemed to acknowledge Falfa as her boss, and she accompanied her faithfully. Even when Falfa picked her up, she didn't appear to mind. I'd watch them from a distance, grinning to myself.

My daughter is cute. The kitten is cute. Put them together, and the cuteness is infinite!

The way Shalsha would hesitantly come up at times like that and pet her on the head or below her chin was also quite nice.

However, by a different standard of evaluation, Halkara was holding her own, too.

"Doughnut, no, don't bite, please. No, just because you can't bite doesn't mean you can claw me!"

When Halkara was walking around indoors, Doughnut would scoot up to her and attach herself to her leg.

Sometimes it seemed like she was attacking her, so it looked as though she might consider Halkara to be lower in the hierarchy than she was. On the other hand, perhaps she just thought of her as a companion. Even with the biting, the attacks clearly weren't serious.

As Shalsha put it, "The way you act toward your parents is naturally different from the way you act with your friends." That seemed like the correct interpretation to me as well.

In addition, maybe because she was a wildcat instead of an ordinary cat, Doughnut was very active and had to be taken for walks in the highlands. Since Halkara went off to work as the president of her factory, Laika and I often ended up in charge of the walks.

It was fun just to watch Doughnut run through the open fields in the brisk air.

They say that keeping pets is good for the soul, and I think I know what they mean.

One day, when Halkara had the day off, we decided to go for a walk nearby as a family with Doughnut.

We were so enthusiastic about it that we packed box lunches for all of us.

"Wait! Wait!" Falfa called, running after Doughnut. We followed them at a leisurely pace.

"Doughnut has gotten really used to living here."

It might have been better to say that we'd gotten used to life with a kitten.

"You're right. We will have to give a bit of thought to the future, though."

Laika, ever the honor student, was looking serious now, too.

"What do you mean?"

"Wildcats grow so large they can't be compared with ordinary housecats. When she's full-grown, we won't be able to keep her indoors any longer."

"I see. The 'growing pet' problem, hmm?"

In Japan, I'd seen a news story about someone whose pet turtle had gotten too big for them to keep. Turtles live for decades, so you can end up with grim situations such as the human getting old and having to part with the pet because they can't handle it any longer.

"The highlands are vast, so we'll be able to stay close to Doughnut as long as possible!"

When Halkara spoke, her voice was a bit on the loud side.

She was wearing the "mature working adult" face she wore when she was at work.

"We've lived with Doughnut too long now, and I'll take care of her. I'll take responsibility."

"Mmm-hmm. I don't intend to send her away, so don't worry."

Just then, we heard Falfa shout. "Aaaaaaaah!"

It wasn't tense enough to be a scream, but it was obvious that something had happened.

"Falfa?! What is it?!"

When we ran up to her, there was a big wildcat, more than two meters in length.

The wildcat and Doughnut were gazing at each other.

The adult wildcat was fairly thin, and its body was muddy and dirty. Even so, its legs were stretched out firmly and planted on the ground, as if it had forgotten it was tired.

Before long, the big wildcat slowly approached Doughnut and began licking her.

"That's a parental demonstration of affection. There's no mistake—those two are family. The mother's here."

Even if I hadn't heard Shalsha's explanation, I would have known that was the case right away.

The mother wildcat must have been searching for her missing child all this time. Just by looking at her ragged body, you could tell that she hadn't been able to concentrate on anything else.

"Halkara, since her real mother is here, we need to—"

When I looked at Halkara, she was wearing a despondent expression, and I stopped speaking.

Still, I thought, it wasn't the selfish sorrow of a child. The expression on her face was a mature one.

"So this is good-bye."

As she gazed at the two cats, Halkara murmured quietly.

Maybe the mother wildcat was very intelligent, or maybe she was exhausted, but when Falfa told her there was food back at the highland cottage, she obediently followed Doughnut.

It was possible that Doughnut had told her mother about the food.

In front of the house, the mother noisily scarfed down her meal and regained her energy without incident.

However, there were many people in my family who couldn't be genuinely happy about that.

Since the mother had come, that meant it was time to say good-bye.

After the wildcats had completed an exchange only they could understand, they both turned their tails toward the house. Doughnut's real home was wherever her mother was, not here.

"Doughnut, don't go! Doughnut!"

Falfa called her name over and over; she was crying. I thumped her lightly on the head.

"You wouldn't like it if you and I got separated, would you, Falfa?"

"No…"

"It's the same for Doughnut. If she has a mother, then she'd rather be with her."

Falfa nodded, rubbing at her eyes with her hands.

To be honest, I was more worried about Halkara than about Falfa. After all, she'd liked Doughnut enough to bring her home.

Halkara had stooped down and was quietly waving a hand.

Oh. She was at Doughnut's eye level.

"Good-bye, Doughnut."

Halkara looked far older than I did. Her farewell contained the maturity of an adult and a sense of distance. However, that only meant that something special was happening to Halkara right now, and I didn't know if it was a good thing. If you had to act like an adult all the time, it would wear you out mentally, I was sure.

Then Doughnut spun around to face us.

She trotted right up to stand in front of the crouching Halkara.

"Doughnut, you're going the wrong way."

Halkara and Doughnut gazed straight into each other's eyes.

Doughnut gave a small mew, then began to lick Halkara's hand. Even though she'd bitten her constantly before.

"Oh, that tickles. It's a bit dull when it doesn't hurt, isn't it?"

When she spoke, Halkara's voice was slightly thick.

As if in return for the licking, she petted Doughnut's head.

It was probably about fifteen seconds. After that, as if she'd thought it was time, Doughnut returned to her mother. Any longer, and the mother wildcat would have gotten worried.

"Animals have feelings, after all. She probably wanted to express her gratitude," Laika said, her expression quiet and serious. Yes, she was probably right.

"You're welcome to stop by the factory again, you know? I'll be waiting for you."

Doughnut mewed, as if she'd understood the words.

"I just saw what a big shot Sis Halkara actually is." Rosalie looked impressed as she hovered. "She is a big-sister type, after all. She isn't like your daughter."

It was probably true that Falfa was still a child.

"You're right. She's an adult. Well, as Falfa's mother, I'd have mixed feelings about it if she got too mature, so I think this is just about right."

Take care, wildcats.

One week later.

"Madam Teacher, I brought somebody home with me!"

Halkara was holding a creature that looked like a fox kit.

By the way, it was gnawing on her hand again.

"Look at how much he likes me. I'll just have to be his mother!"

At that point, Shalsha came up rather hastily.

"That breed of fox is the potential carrier of a disease that only elves can catch. It's better if you avoid touching it too much."

It's already bitten her good!

"Halkara, put that one back where you found it! Then go disinfect your hand with medicine!"

That dashed any possibility of our acquiring a new pet.

The End

AFTERWORD

It's been a long time. This is Kisetsu Morita!

And this is Volume 2 of *I've Been Killing Slimes for 300 Years...*!
Once again, lots of new characters made appearances, and Azusa's surroundings have gotten even livelier!

Please treat Rosalie the ghost, Vania the leviathan, and Pecora the demon king with affection! A big thank-you to Benio, who drew the illustrations!

All right, there are lots of things I have to report this time.

First, Volume 1, which came out in January, has been picked up by a whole lot of people! They tell me it's the top-selling GA Novel in history! It was such a shocking idea that I seriously didn't believe it at first, even when my editor told me about it. I have nothing but gratitude for everyone who bought it! Please keep on giving Azusa and the others your support!

In addition, thanks to you, they've decided to turn it into a comic!
The vehicle is GanGan GA, and the artist is Yuusuke Shiba! Please look forward to it!

I really can't wait to see how Azusa and the others are going to move!

Finally, here's a brief preview for *I've Been Killing Slimes for 300 Years... Volume 3!*

- With the addition of a new family member, the blue dragon Flatorte, the house in the highlands grows even livelier!
- Laika and Flatorte have a cookie bake-off with the prestige of dragons hanging in the balance!
- For some reason, Falfa the slime spirit goes back to being a slime?!
- Everyone hunts a boar and eats wild game together!
- A false Azusa, the Witch of the Highlands, appears?!

—Plus a whole lot more! It's scheduled to go on sale in July!

As Azusa and the others play out more and more stories, I feel as if I've gotten used to the house in the highlands and life in the demon lands. People often talk about how characters "just move on their own," and I think this might be what they mean.

I'm still serializing the story on *Shousetsuka ni Narou (So You Want to Be a Novelist)*, and although I'm the author, even I'm not really sure what's going to happen next.

I suspect that the vicinity of the house in the highlands is going to keep getting livelier and livelier, so please continue to give us your support!

Kisetsu Morita